Road Side Crosses

A NOVEL

Darleen Turner

Copyright © 2013 by Darleen Turner.

Library of Congress Control Number:		2013902464
ISBN:	Hardcover	978-1-4797-9188-0
	Softcover	978-1-4797-9187-3
	Ebook	978-1-4797-9189-7

All rights reserved. No part of this book may be reproduced or transmitted in any form or by any means, electronic or mechanical, including photocopying, recording, or by any information storage and retrieval system, without permission in writing from the copyright owner.

This is a work of fiction. Names, characters, places and incidents either are the product of the author's imagination or are used fictitiously, and any resemblance to any actual persons, living or dead, events, or locales is entirely coincidental.

This book was printed in the United States of America.

Rev. date: 04/15/2013

To order additional copies of this book, contact:
Xlibris Corporation
1-888-795-4274
www.Xlibris.com
Orders@Xlibris.com

Dedication

Roadside Crosses is dedicated to all the families that have had the tragic pain of putting up a cross in remembrance of a loved one whom they have lost in some horrific accident. Your pain we share, and your loss we share. Your memories will always be yours to hold within your hearts to cherish.

We would also like to say thank you to all our emergency workers. Their job is hard at the best of times, and we all appreciate knowing that if it is our turn to be in the predicament that we are calling on your help. Please let God be with us and riding with you.

Go and Godspeed!

Chapter 1

"STOP DADDY, STOP."

The tears ran down her cheeks as she turned away and kept watching over her shoulder. So many times she had said the same thing to her father, but it was like he never heard her. Jessy couldn't understand that people could be so cruel. Why wouldn't you stop the pain and suffering of another living soul? How can you just carry on like it meant nothing to see pain? After five minutes had passed, Jessy was wiping the tears away as she asked, "Why didn't you stop, Daddy?"

"Now, Jessy, we have been over this a few times. It's always too late to stop. I'm sorry if I hurt you by not stopping, but really, there is nothing I or you can do. Some things are out of our hands, and if the good Lord wished for it to be any different, I'm sure there would be a sign of some kind."

"Maybe if you would stop just once when I asked, we would see a sign from God."

"Now, Jessy, when you get older, you will understand that there is a reason why men are this way and why women and girls are the way you are. But until then, please don't ask me to just stop whenever you think I should. There are times when fathers know best."

"Well, Mommy knows all the time, and she says for me to keep asking you to stop and one day you will and you will see how good I am."

"Oh, my dear girl, Daddy knows just how good you are, and you always have been. Now can we finish our day on a happier note?"

From the time Jessy was old enough to know when something was hurt, she wanted to fix it. It didn't matter whether it was a bug or a bigger animal.

Jessy was from a split home, so when she would be on a trip with her dad going back home and there was some animal lying on the side of the road, she would always ask her dad to stop so she could see if there was anything she could do to fix it. At first Jessy would get so upset because her dad wouldn't stop. She learned as she got older it was because he knew they were already dead, and Jessy couldn't do anything for them.

This ended up being Jessy's passion, and so she went on to becoming a veterinarian. Jessy took every class she could take and spent all her waking hours studying. Once Jessy was done doing that, she then became an emergency medical technician, better known as a paramedic. Jessy lived for this, and it was all she cared about. Her passion to help the hurt was way beyond anyone's comprehension.

On one of their trips, when Jessy was fourteen, there was a wounded great horned owl flopping around on the road. Someone had hit it but not hard enough to kill it. The owl was just a young bird learning to fly. This was one time when Peter did stop as Jessy cried out, "Stop, Dad!"

Peter threw his coat over the owl so he could scoop it up and put it into Jessy's hands. The owl had a broken wing. They were not to be kept in captivity, so Peter called the wild game office and explained to them what had happened. The officer said he would send them a paper to fill out allowing them to keep the bird until it was healed. He then gave her some instructions on feeding the bird, and wishing Jessy luck in caring for the bird. Jessy called the bird Duke.

It didn't take long before the day came for Jessy to turn Duke back into the wild. It was a rewarding day for her. Jessy had saved the poor thing from suffering and got it back into flight. Duke had hung around for a few days waiting for Jessy to feed him as he had gotten used to easy food. She didn't want the bird to depend on her anymore, and it was hard for her to put Duke on ignore, but he finally gave up waiting for food and left. Every now and then, there is an owl that flies overhead, and they're not sure if it's Jessy's patient or just another owl. Jessy swears it's Duke.

Jessy's second patient was a red fox. It too was a pup, probably around six months old. It had its paw caught in a trap and was dragging the trap along with it as it tried to run away.

Peter had a neighbor who had been bothered by foxes getting his chickens, so Jessy knew where this fox had been. Once it was sedated and the trap removed, Jessy found that the paw had to be removed, and so she took it into the vet as she wasn't set up for that kind of treatment yet. The fox would have a limp but would do fine with what it had left. She thought of the story about the little engine that could. So she called him Red. She knew this little fox had plenty of spunk to get it through whatever was in its way.

She kept him for eight weeks then when she was satisfied that he could hunt on his own, she turned him back to the wild. He too stayed around for the easy meals. Spoiling him came easy as he was so beautiful. Jessy would take food out on horseback and drop it off away from the farm so he would follow. Then one day he just never came back. They had heard neighbors talking about the fox that had no foot from time to time, so she knew he was still doing well on his own.

Sharon would remind her that she was young and should live a little. Jessy's reply was always the same: "I have lots of time, Mom, but hurt people and animals don't."

Sharon would back off after talking to Peter and having been told so many times.

"Be grateful, Sharon, that she isn't causing you and I a headache. Coming from a split home, I think Jessy is doing very well for herself, and neither one of us should complain. Do you see the kids out there from broken homes, Sharon? Be thankful our daughter hasn't chosen to live in self-pity and drugs. She has moved on from our divorce."

"I know you're right, Peter. But she is missing out on all the young-people doings."

"Jessy is doing what Jessy has always loved to do, and that is doctoring something. Remember when she brought home that cat that she saw get hit? I would have hit it on the head and done away with it. Not Jessy, and because of her love and caring, that cat survived. How? I don't know, but our daughter has the touch, and we should be proud and encourage her to continue, not try to hold her back."

"I don't want to hold her back. I don't want her to be sorry and regret not living and doing the things young people are supposed to do."

"Suppose to do? By whose books, Sharon? Yours. It's because you want her to get married and have grandchildren for you. That, I would think, is more like it, and very selfish on your part."

"Don't you want grandchildren, Peter?"

"Someday, when it happens. I don't expect Jessy to give up her dream and her life to make me a grandfather. I'm sure when she is ready, she will do just that. Have you ever thought that just maybe seeing how we turned out, and our marriage, it might have scared her away from doing the same thing?"

"It wasn't all that bad!"

"No! Then why haven't you or I made another commitment to anyone else? I will tell you why. We have scared ourselves from having another relationship. So please, just leave Jessy alone and let her enjoy her life the way she wants."

"She has to be lonely."

"I'm sure if that were the case, we would have heard about it and she would have done something to change it."

"I guess you're right."

"You know, Sharon, if you want grandchildren around, why don't you take in babysitting? There are many young girls who would love the break from their children."

"It's not the same, Peter, and you know it. Besides, I have my business to run."

"No, but just maybe a few days with them, you won't try to hurry Jessy into it either."

"Oh, Peter, you're hopeless."

"I know. That's why we are divorced. I have to go now, we will talk later." He hung up.

"Damn him," Sharon said as if it was his fault Jessy didn't seem interested in a relationship. But was Peter right? Was it because their marriage fell apart? Sure, they had their fights but nothing so mean and nasty that it should have scared Jessy in any way of wanting a relationship.

Sharon still had feelings for Peter, and if she were to be honest with herself, she knew deep down she still loved him, and that was why she had never moved on. Sharon would never love another man as she loved Peter. Although they couldn't live together, they still got along and spent quality times together and family time with their daughter.

This made Sharon wonder if it was the same for Peter. Was that why he has never gotten involved with anyone else? Did he still love her? This made her feel a like a young girl wishing for her first love to call back.

Peter and Sharon have been divorced now for five years and still stayed friends through it all. They still have their romps in the hay, and perhaps that was enough for them. They were good times, and there was no pressure from either side. When it happens, it was totally out of the blue and was so fulfilling that Sharon wouldn't want it any other way. They were happy with what they have, Sharon thought.

Sharon had not dated another man, and as far as she knew, Peter had never taken another woman to his bed. Now when he is out of town on his cattle trips, Lord only knew what he did, but then it was no concern of hers. After all, they were divorced.

Together they saw their daughter through her education and never blinked an eye. They both made good money, Sharon being a bookkeeper and Peter being a farmer. Yes, he had good years and bad years, but he had always put away for the bad.

Sharon had gotten her bookkeeping right out of high school so she could help Peter with the farm. That was when some of the marriage fell apart. He didn't want to listen to her suggestions. What did she know? She was just a bookkeeper. Now he was willing to discuss those angles with her. Some of it was because they haven't pissed each other off beforehand, so they could talk these things out now. Really, it didn't matter to her. It was his farm, but he liked to include her in his decisions still.

Sharon got to be well known for her bookkeeping, and Peter respected her because of it. She ran her office out of her house that Peter had bought for her after their divorce as her settlement. Sharon was just going to rent, but Peter thought it would be better if they bought the house. It was also a right off for him.

The house was small, but Sharon said that was all she needed, and now with Jessy on her own, Sharon turned her bedroom into her office. She had a sofa bed for whenever Jessy wanted to sleep over, which was only on the holidays that she didn't get out to the farm because she was on call.

After the divorce, Jessy spent most of her time at the farm with Peter. She said it was so she could practice on his cattle. Sharon thought she felt sorry for Peter and was afraid he would be lonely and find another woman. She knew she was content and wasn't interested in another man. But men seem to have to have someone taking care of them. Jessy tried to be her father's chief cook and bottle washer, but she soon learned that her father was better at it then she was.

Sharon liked the fact that she spent so much time out there at first. After all, it was her home, and her father's. With her at the farm, it took Sharon out there many weekends. It only took them a few months for Jessy to accept the fact that her parents had divorced on good terms and the way they were living wasn't hurting anyone. They all fell into a routine that worked for them, and they were all happy.

Jessy didn't tell anyone that her parents had divorced. She felt people would look at her funny. It took her a long time to tell Trisha, and Trisha was like a sister to her all her life.

They had always been seen around town as a family, and that never changed. They always had a good time when they were out together, so in time, Jessy just fell into their relationship as the third party, and all was great. All the holidays were the same.

The only thing that changed for Jessy was the fact that her parents lived in different homes, and at first, she found it hard to be visiting one without the other. She was always worried about hurting one of their feelings. As time went on and she saw it didn't bother either one of them, Jessy was able to relax and totally enjoy her family again.

People thought they had a messed-up relationship, but for the three of them, it worked just fine.

Chapter 2

Running as an EMT held first priority in Jessy's life, and everyone around her knew it. They also knew her second love was veterinarian medicine. It wasn't anything she laughed about or cut attendances short on. So Jessy's life was full, and she didn't have time for relationships and motherhood.

Jessy was grateful that Peter had the farm. It provided her with a place to practice, and her knowledge had come in handy. She had saved Peter many calves and some cows.

She still had one of the horses that Peter used to ride the fence with, up in a sling. He had stepped into a gopher hole and broke his leg. Peter himself would have just shot the horse because it took so much time and trouble to get it healed. This time, he called Jessy to see what she would do with him. Jessy knew he was her dad's favorite horse, and Peter had had him for many years.

She had gone out and sedated the horse because, like humans, they hurt when something is broken. Before the horse fell asleep Peter, and Jessy had put the big tarp strap around his front and around his backside then Peter lifted him with his tractor and hauled him to the barn, where they had hooks mounted on to the rafters. It wasn't anything special, but it would keep the horse off his feet until Jessy got a cast on it then she was hoping to put him into a sling. The only thing they had there that would work for making a sling was a one-ton tote bag that alfalfa cubes had been brought home in. They would still use the big tarp straps that Peter had just to make sure nothing let go.

This took all day to get rigged up and to get the cast on the horse. Jumper was his name, and he seemed to know that Jessy was helping him, and even once the sedative wore off, he stayed calm. He wasn't a young horse, so maybe that made a difference. He handled it all quite well. Both Peter and Jessy were impressed.

"Dad, I will sleep out in the barn tonight."

"You think you really have to do that? He isn't acting like anything is bothering him."

"He is calm, all right, but I would feel better, just in case."

"I will make supper then I will join you."

"Dad, you don't have to do that."

"I know I don't, but when was the last time you and I got to camp out? Could be fun."

Jessy laughed and said, "Okay, Dad, sounds like a good plan to me." She wrapped her arms around his middle and hugged him while asking him, "What's for supper?"

Peter looked at her with a frown and said, "Hey, what else? Pork and beans, for sure. I will see what else I have that's quick."

"Would be great to have fresh bread to go with that hey."

"Yeah, where's your mother when we need her?"

They were both laughing when Peter left for the house. He thought he best go do the supper thing. Jessy was much better at being a vet than a cook. He had learned that a long time ago, and so had she.

Jessy talked to Jumper as she got busy fixing her spot that she would sleep in for the night. Jessy had already gotten her water out of the truck but had wished she would have gotten a thermos of coffee. Jessy was also glad that she was on her four days' off. She knew that her dad didn't have the patience that this would take, but in four days he would be able to take over. Jessy would show him everything he needed to know as far as care. The main thing was to exercise the other legs. That was where the time and trouble came in at.

When Peter came back, he had made biscuits to go along with his pork and beans. Jessy was surprised 'cause he had even made coffee. He had also thrown in the last of the apple pie.

Whenever Sharon went out, she baked up a storm just to see him through until her next visit.

"It must be time for your mother to visit. This is the last of her baking."

"You're lucky she still does that for you, Dad."

"We're lucky she does."

"Yeah, guess so. Hey." Tilting her head to the side, she said, "Dad, will you and Mom ever live under the same roof again?"

Raising one eyebrow, he said, "Don't think so." The way he had said it left Jessy thinking someday it will happen.

"Why not? You spend all the holidays together."

"That's a tough call, but we are happy this way, and it works for us."

"Do you still love Mom?"

He took a few minutes to put his thoughts in order. Jessy thought perhaps she was going to be sorry she had asked.

Then he said, "Yes, that never changed Jessy. We just grew apart. This happens to many couples, but they fight it until they end up hating each other instead of just knowing that it's time to move on. We would sooner be friends and still share our daughter than to fight and one or both of us lose her and her love."

"I would never quiet loving you or Mom."

"That's because we won't give you a reason to." Peter pulled her tightly to his side.

"That is true. You both have supported me all the way."

"Yes, and where did it get you? Sleeping in the barn?"

"Mom!"

"Hi, Sharon, come join us."

"Here, I brought something for a peace offering." Sharon handed over a freshly baked loaf of bread to Peter.

"Umm. Smells great and will go with our supper, kiddo. How did you know?"

"I called to talk to Jessy, and they told me what had happened, so I figured I would find the two of you out here trying to mend a broken horse. I know how you like your pork and beans when you have to hang out in the barn. You always did during calving."

Peter chuckled and said, "Some things never change. Guess I must be reborn from that time when pork and beans were eaten a lot on chuck wagons and cattle drives."

Everyone laughed, and Sharon turned a pail upside down so she could sit down on it. Sharon knew she looked out of place sitting on that pail because she always dressed up. It was because Sharon never wanted Peter or Jessy to be embarrassed of her.

As they were about to enjoy their supper, Jessy's phone went off. Peter and Sharon could tell it wasn't good news. The look on their daughter's face told it all.

"I'm sorry. I have to go in. There has been a multiwreck, and they need everyone available."

"It's okay, sweetheart. You have us under control here. Please be careful, and call us as soon as you can."

"I will." Jessy hugged both of them and left them attending to the broken horse, as Sharon called him. Visions of her parents in the barn for the night made her chuckle to herself as she drove away.

"So did you eat, Sharon?"

"I had lunch about three."

"So will you share my pork and beans with this fresh bread you brought?"

"I would love to."

Peter got out his knife and opened a can of beans. They were the sweet ones that didn't need warming. They were good right out of the can.

When they first started farming, they thought they had to sit out and watch the cows during calving. They had heard about all those horror stories from their neighbors. But over the years Peter and Sharon found that their cows didn't have trouble. Peter didn't use a big bull and he thought that must have been the difference, so there was no need in staying out with cows all night. Jessy did when she was home, but that was because she was playing veterinarian and she enjoyed it.

Sharon lay back in the hay that Jessy had made up for herself after supper, watching Peter tend to the horse. She then realized just how sexy he still was for a fifty-eight-year-old. His body was still firm and strong. Sharon knew why she had never taken up with another man: Peter was all the man she would ever need. With that thought in mind also came thoughts of what the evening could have in store for them. Sharon picked up a piece of hay, putting it in her mouth to chew as she had seen Peter do so many times.

Chapter 3

This wreck was a real horrifying one. A truck with two men in it had tried to miss a moose. It swerved into the other lane, catching a minivan with a family of four in it, causing it to spin around and then have the vehicles behind them pile into them. The drivers said it all happened so fast they didn't really have a chance to react.

The two men in the first truck ended up in the ditch while the minivan was being sandwiched between other vehicles. The two men didn't have anything but bumps and bruises.

The ones that piled into the minivan had more serious cuts and a couple of broken bones. Jessy helped get them all stable, and some had been taken to the hospital. She was sick to the stomach just knowing that they hadn't gotten to the ones who would be the worst injured.

Everyone was waiting to get to the minivan that had been sandwiched between all the cars. At this point, no one knew how many there were in the minivan or how bad they would be hurt. No one thought it would be good news. Once the people from the other vehicles had all been cleared away and the tow truck pulled the other vehicles away, it was time for the Jaws of Life to take over.

The driver's side of the van had been completely smashed into the other side. The chances of anyone surviving this would be a miracle. Jessy's heart was pounding so loud in her chest with fear, she felt like she would pass out. She stood watching as the Jaws of Life started to pull the van apart. They needed to get it away from the victims inside so they could take the doors off.

When the Jaws of Life had finished opening up the minivan, they found that the father and son were dead. Jessy had climbed into the backseat where they had removed the young boy's body from.

The little girl still held her teddy bear tightly in her grasp. Jessy was able to get her vitals and an IV started on her. The little girl was breathing but barely, and they weren't sure if they would get her out in time or what all she had for injuries. Through all the blood, Jessy could tell the girl was blond and about four years old. The boy looked to be about seven.

The mother wasn't in any better shape than her daughter. It was a young family, and probably a happy one that morning.

After another half hour, the mother and daughter were sent to the hospital, but no one expected them to make it. It turned Jessy's stomach to see such a horrible sight. She knew someday it would come to this. She had already dealt with some terrible accidents, but nothing like this one. It shook her to the core.

Jessy would find out what the little boy liked to do and what the father had done for a living. She wrote poems for all her accident victims. She liked to keep notes on everyone. Somehow it made her feel like she knew them a little bit better.

ROAD SIDE CROSSES

Jessy also made white crosses for all their victims and would inscribe their names into them. She would go back out to the scene and put them up for their families. She felt that, that was where their spirit left them and so that was where it should be marked. To her, a graveyard was so impersonal. It just made it easier for everyone to be able to gather to say their final good-byes.

Jessy would keep close contact with the hospital and see how the mother and daughter made out. Most of the EMT stayed away once they delivered. They said they didn't like getting close and personal. It made their job to hard.

For her, personal was the only way to be. Jessy liked to know what happened to the victims that she helped out. It was like if she knew one pulled through, then she had done her job. It was all worthwhile. It made her want to go on.

Jessy went back to the station and changed her clothes and headed back to the farm. After all, she had another patient that was in need of her attention. Getting back to the farm and sliding the barn door open, she was surprised, somewhat shocked, yet pleased to find her mom sleeping in her dad's arms. Jessy could only think of one thing.

Aw, that's so sweet.

She just went about her business and was checking the horse out when her parents woke up, acting like they were kids that just got caught with their pants down.

"Hey, don't look so worried. I'm glad I didn't come back and find one of you with the pitchfork stuck into you." Her parents never fought that bad, so it was a little overexaggerated, but she wanted them to relax. After all, they were her parents and were adults.

"I would never do that to your mother!" Peter said as he leaned over and kissed Sharon on top of her head and got up, brushing the hay off himself.

"I know, Dad. Jumper seems to be calm still this morning. Will you help me with his exercise now?"

"I sure will." Then Peter turned to Sharon and asked, "Would you be so kind as to go make our daughter some breakfast and coffee? She looks like hell." He reached out to take Sharon by hand to help her up off the hay bed that they had shared.

"Sorry, it was a rough night."

"I will gladly make coffee and breakfast for everyone." Sharon too had to brush herself off.

"Thanks, Mom."

"You're welcome, sweetheart, and I will text you when it's ready."

Peter and Jessy got right into exercising Jumper's legs. Peter had to lower the hoist they had him on. Jessy wanted it so his feet barely touched the ground. She didn't want any weight put on the broken leg. She had hoped to be able to put a walking cast on him later on. Jessy knew he wouldn't be able to move the broken one very much as she had put the cast as high up as possible.

They lifted and moved the other three legs back and forth and rubbed them down for an hour. In a few weeks, she would probably let him stand on all four depending on how quickly his bones mended at his age. Jessy would borrow the portable x-ray machine again from the vet clinic and check him out before allowing him to stand on it.

"Do you think he will heal well enough to ride again, Jessy?"

"You bet, Dad." Jessy fed him sweet feed mixed with aloe. She was worried that maybe he wouldn't like it, but Jumper was more human than horse.

Jessy was also a big believer in natural medicine, and she was feeding Jumper an aloe vera plant. Her grandfather ate it all the time and lived a long healthy life. It would help heal the leg from the inside out.

There was lots to be said about aloe. Jessy also drank it daily, and she was sure that was why her skin was so beautiful. She was never bothered with skin problems. Jessy never wore much makeup, except to highlight her eyes. Her dad always called her his pretty tomboy. There was nothing boyish about her. Jessy knew that Peter and Sharon were very proud of her and all she had become.

Sharon had called them up to the house for breakfast, and everyone was enjoying it.

"Mom, Trisha had a baby girl."

"Trisha? I didn't know she had gotten married."

Jessy looked at Sharon with a frown then said, "Mom, you don't have to be married to have a baby these days."

"Sorry, I guess not. How are they? Why had she not told us?"

"Good, I hear. I want to go next weekend to see them. Do you want to come along?"

"I would love to. Where is it that she moved to?

"Barrhead."

"Yes, I recall that now. Sure, I will come for a drive, so long as your father is going to be okay here alone with his broken horse."

"I will be just fine, Sharon, you go with our daughter. It will do you good to go somewhere. You have become such a hermit."

"Sorry, but everything I love is here. Why do I need to go anywhere else?"

"To see different things, Sharon."

"Yeah, look who's talking."

"I go to more places than you."

"Only if it has something to do with the cattle."

"Trust me, there's more there than just cattle."

"Oh, you're impossible, Peter."

Peter slapped Sharon's butt as he walked by. "Yes, I am," he said, chuckling to himself.

Jessy had to laugh at her parents. Sometimes, you would think they were still married. It was moments like this that made her want to come home. She enjoyed being around her mom and dad.

"After breakfast, I'm going shopping to buy a teddy bear. Does anyone need anything from town?"

"I don't need anything. How about you, Peter?"

"Nope. Me neither." Peter and Sharon both thought Jessy was buying a teddy bear for Trisha's little girl.

It took some time to find a bear that might pass. Jessy knew that some kids had favorites and wouldn't accept anything else. This made it very hard to deal with those children.

"Do you want a pink ribbon or blue?"

"Oh, I don't know!"

"Was it a boy or a girl?"

"I don't know that either. I'm guessing a boy."

"When was the baby born? Perhaps I could call the hospital and find out if you have a name?"

"Thank you, but this is for an older child who has lost her teddy bear."

"Okay. Why don't I give you one pink and one blue, and you can put on it whichever the child wants."

"Yes, that would do fine. Thank you."

Gosh. Jessy never knew buying a teddy bear would be so hard. She hadn't even thought about whether it would be male or female. Who would really care? It was just a teddy bear. Pink, blue, boy, girl—a teddy's a teddy.

The woman was helpful, and Jessy was grateful for the eye-opener on buying teddy bears. So she grabbed a white one with a pink ribbon to take to Crystal Marie.

Snuggling it, she felt an awe come over her like none other. Yes, teddy bears do have a special place in one's heart. Yet Jessy could never remember having a teddy bear.

Chapter 4

Jessy had found out that the victims' names were Raymond Helix and David, his son's name. Raymond was a steel worker, and David loved to race dirt bikes. They were just getting back from Smokey River where David had taken third in a race. So on Raymond's cross, she would have a small welding torch engraved into it. On David's, she hung a white ribbon that read "First with God" and a helmet with kneepads and elbow pads. Jessy had soaked them in urethane to protect them from the weather.

The mother, Verna, and little Vicky were holding their own, and the doctors figured that they should both pull through if they made the next seventy-two hours. So Jessy found herself sitting in the little country chapel that was just outside of town. Jessy sat there saying prayers for Raymond, David, Verna, and little Vicky.

Jessy didn't know if praying really helped although she had heard that the power of prayer was a very strong element in many cases, so she would give it a damn good shot. It was too late for Raymond and David, but a small prayer for them didn't hurt.

Jessy found herself there on a daily basis, and then she got the news that both mother and daughter were going to be just fine. Other than dealing with their loss, their health issues were healing well. Some would take time to completely heal, but that was to be expected for the injuries that they had sustained in the accident.

Jessy felt good that what she had done helped that little blue-eyed blonde. Jessy was going to see the little girl and was taking her a new teddy bear. She had tried to find one just like the one she still had clasped in her hands at the time of the wreck. The little girl's was covered in blood and was thrown out before anyone had thought about how attached she might have been to her bear.

The one Jessy found was just a bit bigger, and it was a darker brown than the little girl's had been. As Jessy knocked on her door, she peeked in. Vicky was lying facing the window and didn't move, so Jessy thought she was asleep. Jessy set the teddy bear quietly at the foot of Vicky's bed and was turning around to leave when she heard, "Thank you."

It was a very faint whisper, and Jessy was glad there hadn't been any other noise because she would not have heard the little girl. Turning around, she saw Vicky had picked up the teddy bear and was looking at him.

"You're welcome, Vicky. How do you feel today?"

Vicky just lifted her shoulders and didn't say any more.

"I'm sorry your teddy bear got thrown out. This was the only one I could find like yours."

Vicky sat playing with the pink ribbon around the teddy's neck then said, "Rupert was very old. He was Mommy's teddy bear when she was little. She gave him to me when she went back to work. She said he would keep me company while she was away."

"Oh no. I'm so sorry, Vicky. Maybe I can see if we can find him. What does your mommy do for work?"

"Mommy is a teacher, and Rupert was my best friend in the whole world, He always listened to me."

This was too much. Rupert wasn't just any damn teddy bear. He was a teddy bear with a history. Jessy knew that come hell or high water, she was going to find that teddy bear.

Jessy had spent an hour with Vicky and found she was a girl of very few words. Jessy did all the talking. She could imagine there were lots of questions going on inside Vicky's little head. She would probably need Rupert to talk to as well as some counseling at some point. Most accident victims do. It was a good thing her mother was a teacher because she would have helped at her disposal. Schools always provide counseling for victims.

When Jessy left Vicky's room, she went right to the cleaning staff and asked what happened to the teddy bear. The one woman knew which bear Jessy was talking about and said it would be out in Bin 6 and it had not been taken away yet.

"Do you have more of those?" Jessy asked, pointing to the rubber gloves the woman had on her hands.

"Yes, we do."

"Could I bother you for a pair?"

The woman went to get Jessy a pair of rubber gloves and came back with a mask as well.

"Here, you might want to wear this. You know what blood is like. Good thing it has been cold. It shouldn't be rotten and have no flies."

"Thank you." Leaving her standing there, Jessy headed out back. Lifting the lid of Bin 6, she thought, *Wow, where do I start?*

Taking a deep breath, she thought, *One bag at a time, I guess.* So taking each bag out, she dumped it onto the ground and rummaged through it. Jessy had a few people ask what she was looking for but no takers in helping. Her hands were cold inside the rubber gloves, and after two hours, she had a visitor come out. It was Peggy, the woman who gave her the rubber gloves and mask.

"Here is a hot chocolate. I didn't know what you took in your coffee, so I thought I couldn't go wrong with this."

"Well, thank you. Black coffee would have been fine. I sure wouldn't have complained. This is great."

"I figured you hadn't had any luck in finding the bear, so you should be getting cold by now."

"I hope this is the right bin because there are a lot of bags in here."

"I doubled checked after you left."

"I didn't know you kept records of where the garbage went."

"Yes, we have to in case something comes up missing in that week."

"I'm glad because it should make this a whole lot easier than having to go through all of these." Jessy waved her hands over the bins.

"What's with the bear?"

"He doesn't happen to be just a bear. He is one with a very important past, and he plays a big role in a little girl's future. I think she is going to need him badly in the days and months to come."

"Is that the little girl in room 20B?"

"Yes, it is. Her name is Vicky."

"I heard that her father and brother were killed, and her mother isn't talking."

"Do you know if the mother goes to see her daughter?"

"I'm told not. She doesn't respond when they talk to her about the little girl."

"Sad. I did not know that. Maybe they should take Vicky to see her mom."

"Hey, that isn't my call," Peggy said as she put her hands up in an "I give up" fashion. "I must go back in. My break is almost up. I will come help you when I'm done if you haven't found the bear." She turned to leave.

"Rupert."

"What?" Peggy stopped and turned back around, facing Jessy.

"The bear's name is Rupert."

"That alone says he is an old bear."

"Yep, sure does. Thank you for this, Peggy. It helped warm up my hands."

"Good luck."

"Thank you." Peggy went back to work, and so did Jessy. The bags piled up, and it was a good thing the bear was bigger than a needle because it was almost like looking for a needle in the haystack.

Jessy had stopped for lunch and a bathroom break. People came over to her and would say, "What a kind thing she was doing." All Jessy could say was "Thank you." It had nothing to do with kindness; it was the fact that this bear could make a big difference in a little girl's life. Something so small on her part could be the difference between whether this little girl could look at life with a smile and know that there was sunshine ahead. This bear was real to her, so losing it was like losing another family member, and with a distant mother and two deaths to deal with already, she didn't need the third. Perhaps Rupert would bring her some peace. If Jessy could only find him. A hospital goes through a ton of garbage in a day.

Jessy ate lunch fast and took an extra coffee out with her. It was around 4 p.m. when Peggy came outside. She was dressed to jump right in. Jessy had only begun to touch the surface of this bin. They had been at it for maybe fifteen minutes when they were surrounded by many more of the cleaning staff dressed and already to jump in and help.

Jessy was not a sentimental person because of her job, but this brought a lump to her throat, and tears came to her eyes. All she could do was nod thank you.

There were garbage bags dragged out all over the parking lot, and not a word was being said. They had all been head-down-ass-up for the past hour. Then all of a sudden, they heard, "I found him!" being shouted from the far end, and they all stopped and looked.

Sure enough, there was Rupert being waved around in the air like a rag. Cheers of glory went up, and the staff started jumping up and down.

The young girl in her early teens went running to Jessy. "Is this the bear?"

Jessy reached out with shaking hands to take Rupert. To her, he had become more than just a teddy bear.

"Yes, this is Rupert. Thank you." A lone tear she had been holding trickled down her cheek.

"You're welcome. I'm glad to have helped out that little girl, and you."

"I'm glad you helped out as well. What is your name?" Jessy asked as she wiped the tear that had gotten away from her.

"Cindy."

"Well, Cindy, I will be sure to tell Vicky that you were the one who found Rupert." Jessy felt the need to hug the girl, and with that, she left to help the others toss the bags back into the bin.

Taking poor Rupert home and soaking him in baking soda water to get out the blood before putting him into the wash, Jessy prayed that he wouldn't fall apart. Rupert was in bad shape but didn't need any stitching. She could only hope that once the blood was out and he was dried and fluffed up, he would look like his old self again.

Jessy was excited to be able to take Rupert to Vicky in the morning. She walked in with him tucked in behind her back. Vicky just watched as Jessy asked her, "Do you know who has come to visit you? He was lost and so scared, but I told him that you were waiting for him."

"Who?" was all Vicky would say.

Jessy pulled Rupert out from behind her back.

"Rupert!" Vicky said as she scrambled to the foot of the bed, reaching out to take him.

"I thought you had died with Daddy and David. Oh, Rupert, you don't have to be afraid. I'm here." She had the biggest bear hug on him.

"He doesn't even look like he got hurt."

Vicky looked him over. "Nope, not even a scratch."

"A young girl by the name of Cindy found him."

"I'm glad, 'cause he would have been scared all alone."

"I think so too. He was very happy when I told him I knew where you were."

"Thank you."

Jessy didn't think anyone would be taking that bear from her grasp again. "You're welcome, Vicky. Now I must go. I will leave you and Rupert to visit. I think you have lots of catching up to do. I will come and see you tomorrow."

"Okay." There was no doubt that was one happy little girl. Whether she would sit and talk to Rupert or just be happy cuddling him, only time would tell.

Jessy wanted to take the cleaning staff out for pizza for their help and let Cindy know just how happy she had made the little girl in room 20B.

Chapter 5

The following week was busy for Jessy. It had snowed, and of course, no one slowed down, so there were many minor callouts. Nothing she couldn't handle. It was frustrating to see how silly people could be when the first snowstorm hits for the season. Jessy was amazed that more pedestrians weren't run over. There were still kids riding their bikes to school, and she couldn't believe that on the second day of snow, someone had run over a young boy.

Jessy had gotten up that morning feeling great and knew she had one more day to put in, and then she would be off to see her friend/sister and her baby. She always thought of Trisha as her sister. They had been joined at the hip since they started school. Trisha had to move away, and this was hard on Jessy for a while. Coming to terms with the fact that Trisha would go on and have a life without her hurt deeply. At one time, Jessy had thought about moving to where Trisha was, but she couldn't leave her dad and mom behind.

Time made things a little easier and in time she was okay with Trisha moving away. They lived on their phones, and Jessy would often ask Trisha why she wouldn't move back. Jessy knew the answer but would always ask. Trisha had moved away from her parents, not them. Jessy knew Trisha loved her still, but she longed for her friend who was also her sister. Her days off weren't starting soon enough. Then she would get to hold a new baby. A new life begins.

Jessy hadn't been at the station fifteen minutes. She had just poured a cup of coffee when they got the call. They didn't know all the details until they got to the school. There were students everywhere screaming. Some were just crying, and teachers were trying to get them into the school away from the scene, but none of the students were budging.

"Oh my god," Jessy said as she saw the feet sticking out from under the car. The snow had already turned red. The bike was well under the car, so it wasn't just a bump, and the student fell over.

"Let us in. Please let us in. Move back, people, we need to get in." Jessy got down to have a closer look. She wanted to throw up. The car wheel was on top of the little boy's head. She felt for a pulse, but there was none, which she had suspected. She dropped her head and said a silent prayer for the little boy.

"Oh my god! Jimmy! Someone has to move the car!" Jessy heard someone yell from behind her. The person was right; someone had to get the car off this little boy's head. He had not been wearing a helmet. Not that Jessy thought it would have helped at all this time.

Jessy looked up at her partner, Ryan. He was as white as the snow. Ryan hadn't been an EMT very long, and Jessy didn't think he was going to be one much longer.

"Ryan, can you please get the jack from the trunk of the car?" Jessy wasn't sure if he could hear her over the woman who was still screaming along with the students. Jessy thought the woman screaming must have been the one driving the car.

"Ryan!" Jessy screamed at him. "Get the damn jack!"

Ryan jumped as if he had been shot, looking stunned at Jessy before what she had asked him to do had registered. Ryan finally got the jack from the trunk of the car. When he got it out, he stood at the side of the car and threw up. He had visions of the child's head under the tire although he figured it was too late for the child. He was going to have a hard time jacking the car up with his hands shaking as bad as they were.

Ryan fumbled around with the jack until he finally got it into place and he was able to get the car off the boy's head. They didn't want to pull him out with all the students still standing there, but having no other choice, Jessy and Ryan slowly pulled the boy's body toward them.

"Ryan, get us a blanket please."

Jessy had already taken his vitals and knew the little boy had died before they got there. She didn't want to cover the boy's body up in front of all these people either. This would not make the scene any easier to take for all who were watching.

No one was moving. The teachers were frozen to their spots as were the students and parents who had witnessed the accident.

This would shake the students and the adults for some time to come. She hoped it would be a good hard lesson for everyone to learn. Snow and bikes and students. Christ, can't people slow down when the weather changes?

Jessy found out the boy was twelve years old. He had just begun to live. His name was Steven. His little sister and mother saw it happen as they were walking a ways behind him. His bike had slipped in the snow when he caught the curb, putting him under the car. The driver panicked and stepped on the gas instead of the brake. This was something that happened so often. Jessy knew it wouldn't help make the driver feel any better, so she wasn't going to waste her breath.

This was not how she wanted to end her four days on, but with this job, you never knew what each shift was going to bring. Ryan and Jessy stayed with the boy. The mother and daughter were taken in the other ambulance to the hospital. The mother they had sedated as soon as they could. The little girl never said a word. They all knew she was in shock. She was wrapped in a warm blanket and was being held by the other ambulance attendant.

Ryan said nothing for the rest of the trip. Jessy thought he was feeling embarrassed because he had gotten sick. Ryan had just turned twenty-six. Jessy, at thirty-three, had seen her fair share, and she too had gotten sick at times.

When they were back at the station and had finished up the paperwork, Jessy made fresh hot chocolate. Taking the two cups, she went over to sit beside Ryan. Ryan sat on the sofa with his head hung, not saying a word to anyone. He never lifted his head or his eyes as she approached him.

"Here, Ryan, have this. It will warm you up, and we haven't eaten today."

"Thank you." This came out in a croaky whisper. Jessy knew he was on the verge of crying.

"Ryan. It's okay to cry. It just means you have feelings, not that you're not a man." She saw the tears trickle down his cheek.

"I could hear his head bones, Jessy, when I jacked the car off of him. God, Jessy, did I kill him then?"

"No, Ryan, you did not. I had already checked. He was dead when we got there. You didn't hear that, Ryan. It would have been the snow crunching under the jack."

"Are you sure, Jessy?"

"Yes, Ryan, I'm positive. We had no choice but to lift it off of him, Ryan. Remember, you took that in training, right? We have to assess the problem then act."

"Yes, I remember. I will never forget it, Jessy."

"In this job, Ryan, there are going to be a lot of accidents you won't forget."

"How do you do it, Jessy?"

"Bad ones I go home and cry about, like today. I won't be able to eat or sleep well for a couple of days. I write in my journal about it. It helps me put things into perspective, and I write a poem for each of my victims."

"You do? Why? How can you write about such things?"

"I will find out about what the little boy was like and what his likes and dreams were. That is what I write about. It will make me feel like I knew him, and it is easier to say good-bye. He is not just a number on a sheet of paper. He is a little boy who was loved by many, and I want to know him. I want to be able to feel, Ryan. I don't want to ever do this job and not have feelings for the people I help, whether they live or die.

"I will get a school picture of him and look at it many times over the next little while. It will give me a better picture in my mind to remember him by than how we found him. I will get one for you, and you study the picture, Ryan. To see a young smiling face staring back at you is a hell of a lot better than the picture you have etched in your head right now."

Ryan looked at Jessy like she was crazy.

"Trust me, Ryan, it works. I have been doing this since I was very young. When my cat got ran over, I would always look at the pictures we had taken because a flattened-out cat with its guts hanging out is not what I want to see in here when I close my eyes at night." Jessy pointed to her head.

"My cat's picture was on my nightstand so I could see him healthy and happy. So for this little boy, we will do the same. I want to see his smiling face, not his head under the tire lying in all the blood."

"That is all I see, Jessy, when I close my eyes. Red snow and flat head. Oh god, Jessy."

"Yes, it will be, until you get a different train of thought. Have you heard of the saying, Ryan, mind over matter?"

"Yes, I have."

"Good, because that is what you are going to learn how to do. Now I'm going to go up to the hospital to see how the mother and sister are doing."

"You are? Why?"

"So I can find out more about Steven, Ryan."

"But, Jessy."

"You don't have to come with me. I understand. I have to do this for myself. It helps me to say good-bye and to move on. You have to be able to say good-bye and move on, Ryan, or this job is not for you."

Ryan just hung his head and cried into his hands. Jessy left Ryan alone with his thoughts and went back to the hospital.

The mother was still sedated, and the little girl who was still sitting at her mother's side was waiting for her daddy. He was out of town when he got the call, so he would be a while. They were new in town, so there was no one to take the little girl home. The nurse would take care of her until her daddy arrived.

Sitting and talking to Rebecca, Jessy found out many things about Steven and what the family did together. Steven loved to play chess. Rebecca said he could beat her daddy all the time. They travelled a lot and had been in Africa until a month ago. Rebecca had just turned seven.

Jessy had found out later that they had adopted Rebecca. That was why there was such a big age span.

When she got home that day, she sat at the table and drew up what she wanted the cross to look like. She was going to put black-and-white checkers squares on it to represent Steven's chessboard.

After she was happy with what she had drawn out and the short poem she had written for him, Jessy called her mom. She told her about the day and to confirm what time she would be picking her up.

"Are you sure you are up to going, Jessy?"

"Yes, Mom. This is what I really need to do, especially now."

"Okay, dear. Love you. See you in the morning."

"Love you, Mom."

Jessy felt drained as she hung up. She was tired but knew she wouldn't sleep well. Looking forward to tomorrow and a new beginning, Jessy had her bath and watched TV until she fell asleep in the wee hours of the morning.

Chapter 6

Sharon and Jessy were on the road by 6 a.m. It was only a three-hour drive, and they wanted to be off the road before it got too busy and they become one of the victims. Jessy felt confident in her 4×4 and her defensive driving. Jessy felt everyone should take a defensive-driving course or maybe a Valium before leaving home.

Jessy was very quiet this morning, and Sharon had noticed it, so Sharon just had to ask. "Sweetheart, are you okay this morning?"

"Yeah, Mom, why?"

"You are so quiet."

"I'm sorry. I was just thinking about Steven and Ryan."

"Who is Steven?"

"The little boy who was killed yesterday."

"Ryan, his father?"

"No. Ryan has been my partner all week."

"Oh! So why are you thinking of him? Is there something we should know about?"

"No, Mom, not like that. Ryan is twenty-six, and he was very upset yesterday. I don't think he is cut out to do this job. I'm worried about him. I hope he will be able to put this accident behind him."

"I remember you having some tough ones."

"Yes, I did and still do, but you have to know how to separate yourself and work. I am hoping I can see him through this and that it will help him. I hope he will take what I have learned over the years with him when he moves on. If he does."

"That bad, hey?"

"It made it worse when I asked him to jack the car up off the boy's head."

"Oh my gosh, Jessy, I guess. How can anyone do that?"

"Mom, we have to. We couldn't just leave it on his head. It looked horrible, and there were children all around us. Ryan didn't take that too well."

"I guess not. I wouldn't have either. Oh, Jessy, that poor boy."

"Mom, the boy was already dead. I had checked him when we got there."

"Not that boy. I was talking about Ryan."

"Mom, Ryan is now a man with a big job. So he has to learn to deal with these things or quit."

"Jessy May, don't be like that." Jessy knew she had upset her mother when she got called Jessy May. "Just because you have the heart to be able to help people and not have it bother you to that point doesn't mean that's how everyone should be. Don't get me wrong, I'm so proud of you and how you handle these things. But, honey, I have to be honest with you. I couldn't and I don't care how many pictures you hung up in my face. When I closed my eyes, I would still see the horror of it all."

"You're right, Mom. I have had to do some real brain training to be able to deal with some of these. It's not easy, nor do I forget what it was like my first time. But you train yourself to put it all aside until later. At that very moment, people are counting on your help. So I just dive in and do whatever I can to make them comfortable, and I hope helping them saves them. I still get sick. I think it is more from my adrenalin dropping than anything. Sometimes I get the shakes so bad, when I get back home it takes a couple hours to settled down and get my thoughts under control. I concentrate on what needs to be done at that very moment, not what everything looks like around me. If you look at the whole picture, it is too upsetting. Like yesterday with the little boy. His mother and sister saw it happen along with classmates and teachers. No one could stop it, and no one could help. When we got there, Mom, everyone was screaming and standing around. The boy was dead. What got to everyone was the fact that the tire was on his head. The snow was no longer white. It was red with his blood, and of course, the snow made it look that much worse. It is going to be something they will all remember for years to come. It is a hard lesson to have learned at such a young age.

"So by me not holding it together, I could not have helped anyone. Ryan was almost helpless to me. He froze, he didn't know what to do, he could not focus, and that is very important. Focusing saves lives, Mom. Yes, it was a hard thing for him to jack up the car. We had no choice."

"Oh, dear, I'm sorry. I didn't mean to talk like you were heartless 'cause I know you're not. You are very good at what you do. You have so much passion for your job. That is why you are so good at it. I could not do what you do, and maybe Ryan can't either."

"He is good at what he does. He just has to learn to stay focused, and I hope I can help him with that."

"I'm sure if anyone can, it will be you, dear."

"Thanks, Mom."

"Oh, honey, I have so much respect for what you do, and I hope that if Peter or I are ever in that kind of situation, we will have someone as good as you, taking care of us."

"There are many good EMTs out there, Mom, so don't worry. They never put two green horns in the same unit."

"That is good to know."

"It is sad to know that so many of these accidents could be prevented if people would pay attention to what is going on around them. You know how many times we hear. I never saw them. I want to scream at them and ask them what the hell are they doing behind the wheel if they aren't aware of what is going on around them. I know sometimes road conditions are at fault. Even some of them can be prevented if people drove according to the road conditions."

"You're right, Jessy. We have seen a lot of that over the years, and you think to yourself, 'What a fool.'"

They got to Trisha's place, and she and the baby were just getting up from their nap. Sharon took the baby and fed her while the girls got caught up on all their news. After the ride and the all the talk about accidents, it was refreshing to hold a new life in her hands and to be able to forget the horrible happenings of the day before.

Crystal Marie was a living doll. She had a head of dark hair, and at this time, her eyes were a dark blue. Chances were they would be brown. Trisha was dark, and her daughter looked like her. Keep in mind no one but Trisha knew what the baby's father looked like.

Sharon was going to get her fill of holding and fussing over a baby. She threw her digs into Jessy about making her a grandmother. She also told her not until she married. Sharon knew deep down that if Jessy were to have a baby on her own, she wouldn't care. It would just mean that she herself would have to help out more. Like Jessy had told her, today they don't have to be married to have a baby.

Sharon knew that was so true. She had heard of women going to the sperm bank to get pregnant. They wanted a baby but didn't want a man. To her, that sounded so cold. After all, making babies was to be an enjoyable part of life. Now they have taken the fun out of it and are turning women into baby-making machines. She could not see herself getting pregnant that way. My, how times have changed.

Sharon did hear Trisha tell Jessy that she and the baby's father planned on getting married next summer. They didn't want to marry because of the baby. That doesn't work. So they thought if they took some time and still felt the same by next summer, then they would get married and give the baby her daddy's name.

All weekend long Trisha had to ask if Sharon wanted her to feed or change or bath the baby. The answer was always the same.

"No, dear, I'm fine, and I would be honored to tend to this precious little girl. That is, if you don't mind?"

"Not at all, Sharon, go ahead. If you can't find what you need, call."

"I will, dear." Cuddling Crystal close to be able to take in the baby smells, Sharon was off to do who-knew-what with her. Both Jessy and Trisha would laugh as Sharon left the room with Crystal tucked in under her chin. Sharon was having the time of her life. Trisha did draw the line on nighttime feeding.

"You are my company, and I will not have you getting up with my daughter at 2 a.m."

"I really wouldn't mind, Trisha."

"Sorry, Sharon. I know you wouldn't mind, but I do."

"All right. But I will take over in the morning."

"That is fine with me." Kissing Crystal goodnight, Sharon went to have her bath, leaving the girls to more alone time.

Jessy and Trisha had sat up talking until Crystal woke up for her 2 a.m. feeding.

"I think I will turn in when Crystal goes back to sleep, Jessy. I have enjoyed our time, and I'm glad you and Sharon came."

"Me too, Trisha. We don't do this often enough."

"We are going to start 'cause I want Crystal to know you as I do. You are her family. She needs to know you and your parents as I do so she knows what a loving family is all about."

"We would love to see you and her more often, and be her family too."

Hugging, the girls went to bed.

Jessy laid awake a little while longer, She had wondered if she was missing a lot by not having a baby of her own. Watching her mother with Crystal made Jessy feel sad for her mom. She could tell her mom was ready to be a grandmother, but Jessy didn't know if she was ready for it.

It was a big responsibility and a lifetime commitment. Could she do that? A lifelong commitment—wouldn't that be like getting married? That was something else she wasn't in a hurry to do.

Was she being fair to her parents, especially her mom, by putting her work, her dream before a family? Would her mother still be the same with a baby if it didn't happen for another ten years? Or would she be too old and set in her ways to want grandchildren around?

Jessy had heard from some of her classmates when she was in grade school how terrible their grandparents were. Who has terrible grandparents? Yet there were students who were always excited because the weekend was coming and they were going to see their grandparents. She knew that would be her children. Peter and Sharon would spoil her children, and they too would be looking forward to the time spent with their grandparents. Jessy didn't spend much time with her grandparents, but she loved them. With that thought, she fell off to sleep.

Of course this brought on dreams of grandparents that were from the Wicked West, she was sure. At one point, it woke her up. With a startled look on her face, she had to take a moment to focus and remember where she was. She was not with a wicked witch. Jessy just shook her head and rolled over, going back to sleep. This time, it was a restful sleep.

Chapter 7

The weekend went by fast, and Sharon totally enjoyed spoiling Crystal Marie. She gave Trisha as much free time as she could. It didn't sound like Trisha's parents would be around anytime soon. They were both heavy drinkers and stayed close to home, which everyone felt was a wise choice for them to make. Trisha said there was always fighting whenever her parents were around, so she'd just as soon send them pictures of Crystal Marie and talk to them over the phone. It was easier to hang up than to walk away. Trisha did not want her daughter around her parents when they were fighting, and it seemed to be a never-ending thing.

Trisha herself had left home at fourteen because of their drinking and fighting. She lived with Peter and Sharon until she was sixteen then she moved in with a friend from school. They both had jobs and had done very well. Trisha had taken bookkeeping and accounting. So she had a job that she could do from home. Trisha always liked the fact that Sharon made good money and could be at home. Now with her having the baby, she could do the same thing.

Sharon knew she didn't have to worry about Trisha. Trisha didn't keep in touch as much as she did at first when she first moved away. Once she made friends, she wasn't as lonely anymore. Trisha always knew if she needed them, she just had to call. They had always made that clear to her. It got so that any news Sharon and Peter got about Trisha always came through Jessy.

Sharon was glad that the two girls stayed in close contact. Trisha promised to send pictures, and Sharon had taken a few with her cell phone so she could show Peter when they got home. This was going to be the closest baby they were going to have for a grandchild for some time yet, so she thought she might as well share them with Peter.

The snow had come down hard again overnight, and Jessy and Sharon were glad to be leaving early. Sharon was even more glad that Jessy had a 4×4 and not a small car.

Jessy was telling Sharon about all Trisha's plans for their wedding and that Shawn worked at a trucking company that belonged to his uncle, and his uncle didn't have any children. So Shawn hoped to take over it one day or have one of his own. He worked steady and made sure that Trisha and Crystal had everything they needed.

Trisha grew up with very little, and so big and splashy was not her way. She liked to know they had money in the bank. Her payments would always be made, and there would always be food on the table. Her daughter would have nice clothes but not expensive. Trisha had learned to shop at the bargain stores.

She was not paying $15 for baby sleepers when she could get three pairs for five bucks. She knew her baby would grow out of the clothes fast.

Her clothes she bought there too, and she always looked very nice. Trisha was on the heavy side, but

Sharon had taught her how to dress so she still looked her best, showing her how to dress and look slimmer. Trisha was a daughter that anyone could be proud off. Peter and Sharon made sure she knew just how proud of her they were.

Jessy was driving slower due to the snow, and they saw cars and trucks in the ditches and where some had been pulled out already.

"I'm glad I got my winter tires on last week. I was told that I was a little early for snow, but I wanted to be ready."

"I'm glad you did too. This could be a little scary without good tires."

"Yes, we could be joining them." Jessy pointed to a car that just ran off the road.

"You don't want to stop and pull them out?"

"No, Mom, I don't. I will let the tow trucks do their jobs. It is too dangerous to do that. Everyone travels with cell phones, so they will get the help they need right away."

"Your dad stops and helps everyone out."

"Yes, he does. I wish he wouldn't. People have been killed that way, and I don't want him to be one of the nice guys getting killed helping a stranger."

"To Peter, there are no strangers."

"I know, Mom. Yet he always told me to be careful of strangers. Isn't that ironic?"

"Because you're his baby, and no one had ever mess with his baby 'cause he would be killing mad."

"Do you think Dad will get along with the man I marry?"

"Oh, I think they would have a pretty deep conversation before there was any wedding taking place. Is there someone we should know about?"

"No, Mom, I was just asking. How about you? Would you make his life hell too?"

"Not at all, so long as he made my little girl happy and treated her with respect and kindness. But God help him if he ever hurt you. Between your father and I, there wouldn't be much left to throw to the wolves."

That had Jessy laughing, and Sharon found she had to laugh with her. They were having a good trip home and enjoying their mother-daughter time.

"Oh shit," Jessy said just as they went around a curve. All Sharon could do was put her hand over her mouth. There in front of them was a small car, and it had gone out of control. So Jessy slowed down as fast as she could without causing them problems. They watched as the small car spun around in a complete circle twice before slamming into the end of the guardrail. Sharon could only scream as they saw the guardrail go through the car, ripping it open like a tin can.

"This won't be good." Jessy pulled over as close as she could. "Mom, you stay in here. Mom, are you all right?" The look on Sharon's face had Jessy worried.

"Yes, dear, you go," Sharon said as she waved her hand at Jessy although she felt like she would pass out at any moment.

Jessy ran to the small car, calling 911 on her way. She found two elderly people in the car. They looked to be in their late sixties and early seventies. The woman was lying with her head back against the seat, blood running down all over her face. Jessy thought maybe she had had a heart attack. The gentleman was crying out in pain.

"I have help coming, sir, but it will be about fifteen minutes." So she looked a little closer, and she could see the guardrail had cut through both his legs. Jessy didn't know just how deep it was, but there was a lot of blood already, so she knew it was bad, and after getting a closer look, she could tell arteries had been cut. Jessy knew he was going to bleed to death if she didn't hurry.

"Sir, listen to me please!"

He just cried out louder.

"Please, sir. I'm an EMT, and I'm going to help you. An ambulance is on its way."

Jessy took her scarf off and had to get right down on top of the gentleman to tie it around one of his legs. She was now covered in blood as she stood up. Sharon put a hand over her mouth with what she saw and watched Jessy strip down to her T-shirt then off it came.

"What the hell is she doing?" Sharon climbed out of the truck and ran toward the car. When she got close enough to see all the blood, her stomach turned on a dime and she was throwing up. Jessy hadn't seen her in time to warn her to stay back.

"Mom, go back to the truck and stay there. Help is on the way. Please!"

Sharon just nodded but was frozen to her spot. Jessy had run back to the truck so she could put on a sweater, and she wanted to grab another couple of T-shirts. She wanted to keep her T-shirts for wrapping. They were always good for that as they stretch and tie good.

Jessy grabbed her bag. She never went far without her medic bags for both humans and animals. Jessy knew she didn't have enough wraps in her bag for all the bleeding that was happening.

Jessy was able to tend to the woman. Taking her drinking water and a T-shirt, she washed off the woman's face. Jessy could see she had a bad gash across her forehead that would need stitching. She wrapped one of her T-shirts tightly around the woman's head, hoping to slow the bleeding.

The woman had come to while Jessy was washing her face. Jessy was glad to know she hadn't had a heart attack. The woman kept calling to Don. Jessy figured that was her husband's name. Don had started to pass out off and on, and he was in bad need of a hospital. Jessy had changed the scarf for another T-shirt, not wanting Don to lose any more blood.

Jessy talked to the woman and tried to calm her down, letting her know her husband would be just fine and help was on its way. To Jessy, help wasn't coming fast enough. She felt that Don was losing his battle fast. She would go back and forth, talking to them both and loud enough. She had hoped it would keep them both from going into shock.

In the distance, Jessy could hear the sirens of the ambulance and police cars. She kept saying short prayers for their arrival. *"Please, God, help me here. Help this couple."*

This was one time she felt her praying wasn't going to help. Jessy felt perhaps she didn't have time to get through to God, and this couple would pay with their lives.

Jessy was never so happy to see an ambulance. She showed them her credentials just so they knew she was who she said she was. They told her she had done great being alone. Now they would take over. Jessy saw them using the paddles on Don and knew he was in deep trouble.

Standing by and watching, Jessy kept praying. When the ambulance pulled away, Jessy went back to the truck, and this was one of the times that she started to shake. Jessy shook so bad that she knew she couldn't drive. Leaning on to the side of the truck and looking over at her mom through the window, she found the words wouldn't come out. Taking a deep breath and trying to stay focused, she was finally was able to ask.

"Mom! Are you okay?"

Sharon was sitting with her head down between her knees. "I think so. How about you?"

"No!"

The sound of Jessy's voice had Sharon sitting up fast and looking over at her daughter. Jessy was crying and shaking out of control. Sharon pushed open the truck door, and jumping out on shaky legs, she ran to the other side of the truck.

"Jessy, honey, what can I do?" Sharon took Jessy into her arms and held her tight.

"Can you drive, Mom?" Jessy asked through her sobbing.

"Yes, yes, of course. Come, let me help you get in." Sharon took Jessy around to the passenger side. At this point, Sharon didn't know where she got the strength but was glad to have it. Helping Jessy into the truck, Sharon wrapped her jacket around Jessy's shoulders, hoping to stop her from shaking so fiercely.

"There is a hotel, just five miles down. Mom, we can stay there for the night. Do you think you can drive us there?"

"Yes, of course." Sharon's foot bounced up and down on the gas pedal, giving them a rough start. Sharon knew her daughter was in rough shape, and she thought maybe she should take her to the hospital.

"Jessy, dear, do you need a doctor?"

"No, Mom. all I need is a hot bath and time."

"Okay," It took a little bit more time before Sharon could control her foot.

"I'm sorry for the rough ride, Jessy. I don't know what's wrong with my foot."

"It's shock, Mom, and it makes our nerves react this way," Jessy answered as she shook so hard, her teeth chattered as she spoke to Sharon. For Sharon, it was the longest five miles she had ever driven.

The people at the hotel were great. Because of the storm the night before, they were full, and Sharon was afraid there wouldn't be a room available for them.

People looked at them strangely as they walked up to the front counter. Sharon was damn near carrying Jessy, who was covered in blood, so that alone had people staring at them. Once the hotel staff knew what had happened, they took over and treated them as if they were queens. It seemed like they couldn't do enough, and all Jessy wanted was a hot bath and to go to bed. Her mother would tend to her, so she didn't need all the fuss they were getting from the hotel staff. Then Jessy saw the look in her mother's eyes, and she called one of the girls over as Sharon was calling Peter to let him know where they were and why. She knew he would be worried and waiting for them.

"Please, I don't want you to worry about me anymore. But please help my mother. I am not able to give her what she needs right now, so please tend to her as you have me." Jessy nodded to say yes, she was fine, go ahead now.

"Yes, madam, as you wish."

"Thank you."

After talking to Peter, Sharon now had time to sit and cry and think about what Jessy had told her. She now understood what Jessy was telling her on their way down to Trisha's, about her dealing with whatever she had to then falling to pieces later. It had been hard for Jessy. This had been the first time she had ever dealt with something like this on her own. Sharon had never been more proud of her daughter than she was at that moment. She would make a mental note of letting Jessy know that.

The staff had switched and now were dealing with Sharon. At first she tried to discourage them.

"Mom, please let them help you as they have me, and just relax."

Sharon had noticed Jessy's teeth weren't chattering as hard as they were, so something must be working. She then relaxed and let the staff help her. She had to admit that it was nice having someone fuss over her this way. She couldn't help wish it would have been for another reason.

Chapter 8

Peter was out on his veranda with his morning coffee, waiting for the girls to arrive. They were over an hour late. He knew they would be going slower than yesterday because he knew Jessy would be uptight after what she had just witnessed the day before, and it had snowed more overnight. He also knew the women well, and they were both early risers. So what had happened now? Surely they would have called him. Both women had cell phones, but what if this time it was them in the wreck? What if it was them being helped? Peter had to shake his head and try to clear his mind off these thoughts.

He had paced the floor most of the night, feeling bad that he had not been there for his girls, and with the what-ifs running through his head, it had kept him up. Although he had scolded himself for thinking like he was last night, he was back thinking the same thing this morning. He had always told Sharon and Jessy that talking about what-ifs was a total waste of time, and here, he had wasted a lot of his evening and lost many hours of good sleep doing just that.

As he came back out with his second cup of coffee, he saw Jessy coming down the road. She wasn't breaking any speed limits this morning. Peter headed for the drive and was pulling her car door open as she pulled to a stop.

"How's my girl?" he said as he reached in and pulled her out into a bear hug.

"I'm okay, Dad," she said, trying to get her balance.

"Thank God."

Seeing the look on his face, she knew he had worried all night. "The question is, how are you, Dad? You look awful."

"I'm fine, now that my girls are home." Peter let go of Jessy as Sharon had come around the side of the truck. Turning, he pulled her into his arms and kissed her as though they were newlyweds.

"Wow," was all Sharon could say. Jessy said nothing on the matter, but it warmed her heart to know that her father still cared that deeply for her mother. Perhaps one day they would end up under the same roof again. That was her prayer each and every night. Jessy thought she would lighten the mood.

"How's Jumper, Dad?"

"He's good. Seems to be a little more spunky now. Wants to move all his legs."

"I'm going to go down and check on him."

"All right. I will help your mother get your bags. You are staying over, right?"

"Yes, Dad. I don't work until tomorrow night." She left her parents to deal with whatever was happening. Going to the barn, she couldn't help but smile to herself.

Peter pulls Sharon in for another hug and said, "I just made a second pot of fresh coffee. You up to some?"

"Yes, that would be great."

"Are you staying for the night too?"

Sharon wasn't sure what all she felt in his kiss but knew that Peter was sincerely worried about her and Jessy, and she too wanted to stay with the one person she knew who loved her.

"If you don't mind, I would love to."

"I wouldn't mind a bit. I don't mind saying you girls had me worried this morning too."

"Why's that, Peter?" Sharon said as she put her arm through his and walked to the house with him.

"I thought you girls would have been home over an hour ago. I know you both like to get early starts."

"After what Jessy was through yesterday, when she finally fell asleep—which wasn't until the wee hours into the morning—I just didn't have the heart to wake her at 5 a.m. like she wanted me to. Our daughter was through hell yesterday, Peter. You would have been so proud of her. She totally stunned me with her work ethics. Watching her strip down to her bra to save another's life was something I never expected to see."

"She did what?"

"Oh, Peter, the man in the car had his legs cut nearly off by the guardrail, and Jessy used her T-shirt she had on to tie around one of his legs and her scarf around to stop him from bleeding to death. She finally used another T-shirt 'cause the scarf wouldn't stay tight enough. It did give her time to get another T-shirt. I don't think I would have thought of either."

"Oh my god, Sharon, I didn't know it was that bad."

"I didn't know either, and Jessy didn't miss a beat at the time. The poor girl fell to pieces afterwards."

"Was he alone?"

"No, his wife was with him. She wasn't hurt as bad. She needed stitches to her head, but besides getting a black eye, I think she is going to be just fine."

"What about you, Sharon? Were you able to help Jessy?"

Sharon hung her head and shook it back and forth before saying, "No, Pete, I froze. I didn't do a damn thing but drive us to the hotel. I was throwing up first off, and then I got back in the truck and sat with my head between my knees. I thought I would pass out. Oh, Peter, I felt like such a fool and I let our daughter down."

"Now come, sweetheart. She was lucky you were there to drive for her and to be with her for the night."

"I was totally useless to her."

"Sharon, remember that she took training for this. The most you have dealt with were her minor cuts while growing up. So don't be so hard on yourself. You were with her, and that, by the sounds of things, was the best. She had her mother's love and care when she needed it most."

"How come you can always find the right words to say?"

"I'm glad you think so, but we wouldn't be divorced if that were true." He kissed her on the forehead before saying, "You pour coffee. I will take your bag up stairs to our room."

Looking at him with a bit of a frown, Sharon said, "Okay."

Going over and getting herself a cup and refilling Peter's, Sharon wondered if she was hearing things and if the kiss he had just given her had been a dream, or was it something she was really missing and wanting? Yes, they shared a bed now and again, But never when Jessy was around. It wasn't because of shame or guilt, but they never wanted her to think of them back together just to get hurt when it didn't work out.

This morning Peter had a different attitude, and Sharon wasn't quite sure how to read him. He had knocked her off balance, and it all started with the kiss in front of Jessy. He usually just kissed her forehead or cheek whenever Jessy was around. Then spending the night in his bed with their daughter just down the hall instead of their guestroom, which she usually uses when she comes out. She wasn't complaining, but this was so out of the ordinary that it made her think something was wrong with Peter.

"Hey! You're in deep thought. What's up?" Peter said as he came into the kitchen. He sat down and picked up his coffee but didn't get an answer from Sharon. Cocking his head, he said, "Is something wrong, Sharon?"

"Everything is just fine. Guess I'm just glad to be home and off the roads. It had me a little nervous although our daughter is a great driver."

"I guess that was something for you two to witness. Sorry I wasn't there for you and Jessy."

"It wouldn't have changed what happened and what we saw, Peter."

"No, you're right, but I could have been the shoulder that you were needing."

"Aw, you're so sweet. Thank you. I have done without your shoulder this long. I'm sure I will continue to."

"You saying you don't like my shoulders, Sharon?"

She grinned as she said, "I love your shoulders, Peter. I just don't need to lean on them all the time."

Peter just nodded and smiled as he took a drink of his coffee.

"Peter, what's up with you?"

Just then Jessy came in, so Sharon knew she would have to wait for the answer.

"Hey, Dad, Jumper is doing great. I think he is wanting to walk all right. Funny how they seem to know when they need all the help."

"Yes, he was pretty dependent on you, and he totally trusted you. Animals know if you mean them any harm."

"Oh, and here I thought he just liked me."

"He does like you because you spoil him."

"He's old, Dad. He needs to be spoiled. Something like you," she said as she went over and sat on his knee. She wrapped her arms around his neck tightly before saying, "Did you miss us, Dad?"

Peter pulled her closer. "You have no idea." That was all he said.

Jessy kissed his cheek then got up and poured herself coffee as well as refilled theirs.

Jessy called back to the hospital to find out how Don and his wife were. His wife had been stitched up and was being kept for observation. Don was still hanging in there. Don had lost both his legs, so he was going to be there for a very long time. The good news was they had both survived this long.

Jessy had thanked God that night and thought to herself that was one cross she wasn't going to be making.

Chapter 9

Peter, Sharon, and Jessy watched the old movie on Golden Pond. Jessy said she saw a lot of her parents in them. She hadn't kept up with show business but was quite sure both Henry Fonda and Audrey Hepburn had passed away. Both the actors had made this show a success, and it was one of her mom's favorite. Anytime Sharon felt the need for a feeling of family closeness, she would pull it out. Sharon was a softie, and sentimental movies always made her cry.

Sharon had a great relationship with her parents, and she missed them deeply. Peter's folks were both still going strong, but they lived their lives, busy doing whatever old people do. They visited once a year. They were always off somewhere and said that they would keep the white line rolling under their feet for as long as they could both walk. They travelled Greyhound and saw a lot of country.

Peter never worried about them. He said they knew what they wanted to do and had made plans years before they retired. He was only glad that they had been able to live their dream. So many die before they got to do what they had been waiting to do all those years. Peter found that to be such a shame, yet it was a relief to know his parents were still in good health.

Jessy called it an early night. She was exhausted, and she always slept good in her old bed. It was like safe arms were wrapped around her, and the warmth of her feather bed always brought memories of her childhood. Jessy fell asleep listening to the soft voices of her mom and dad. She could never make out what they were talking about. She knew this was their time to talk, and she would always excuse herself early enough to give that to them. She had done the same when they were a family, living all under the same roof. Respect she would still give them. Who knows, maybe the good Lord was working miracles.

After breakfast Jessy hung out at the barn with Peter while Sharon cleaned up the house. Sharon always liked to put a woman's touch to Peters home before she left. Peter wasn't dirty by any means. Sharon would see to the dust bunnies that he would overlook, and everything always smelled so much fresher when it had a good dusting.

Peter knew he would be left with a shiny house, and some of it he purposely left for her. He knew it made her feel good to be needed still after all these years. He liked what Sharon did to the house, giving it a woman's touch. It made it easier for him when she left 'cause Peter felt her with him for a few more days until the dust took over again. Somehow Sharon always had time to leave Peter a love note, and he said he could never wait till bedtime came around. Peter would wallow in her writing, and he knew he would also be going to sleep with a smile on his face. Peter never went up to read it beforehand. It was his nightcap.

Peter had finally admitted to himself that he was still crazy about that woman, and he could have easily lost them both this weekend. This was making Peter look at his and Sharon's life differently. Sure, they had a comfortable arrangement, but that wasn't enough for him anymore. He had hoped that they had both grown up and matured enough to know they should still be man and wife. He wanted Sharon back home where she belonged, in his bed every night. Not just whenever they found the time. He was wondering if Sharon had thought about her life or theirs after this weekend. Would she come back home if he asked her to, or was she totally content to live this way?

Yes, he had bugged her about other women when he went to the cattle shows, but not once did he take another woman to his bed. Although he had many offers, with him and Sharon being divorced, he felt she was still his wife and would not betray her or her trust. Perhaps if they had had a bad divorce it would have been different, but he never had problems with Sharon, and he never quit loving her. They were just too young and needed space to grow up. He never really knew why they divorced in the first place.

Jessy was dropping Sharon off at home. Jessy was on the night shift, so she wanted to get home and do a few things and perhaps have a nap before going into work.

"Mom, are you all right?"

"Yes, honey, I'm fine. Why do you ask?"

"You haven't said much since we have been back."

"Guess it has just been a busy weekend, that's all. Perhaps I'm tired."

"Hmm, guess so, hey. Well, I hope you get a good night's sleep tonight."

"I will, dear. Thank you."

"Aw, Mom, we forgot to show Dad the pictures of Crystal."

"So we did. We will see him on the weekend. The pictures aren't going anywhere."

"That is true. Thanks for coming, Mom. Sorry it was spoiled by the accident."

"Wasn't your fault, honey, and it spoiled your days off as well."

"It did that, all right. Take care. I will call you later."

"Bye, sweetheart. Talk soon. Hope you have a good shift."

"I do too, Mom. Love you."

"Love you too, dear." Sharon closed the door and waved at Jessy as she drove away.

Jessy got a few of her things done that she wanted to do before catching a nap before going into work. To her surprise, they had a new partner for her when she got into work.

"Hey, Jessy, this is Mitch Acorn. He is taking over for Ryan."

Jessy put her hand out to shake his as she asked, "What happened to Ryan?"

"He is off on sick leave. He has to get consulting after the deal with the little boy."

"I wondered if he was going to be okay."

"You know it's not for everyone, Jessy, so if he doesn't come back, you won't be surprised."

"No, not at all. Thank you, Roy."

"You're welcome, Jessy. I hope you have a quiet night."

"Yeah, me too." Jessy had told them about the accident she and Sharon had witnessed and what she had done.

ROAD SIDE CROSSES

The men just shook their heads at her. They couldn't believe how cool she was with handling the accidents that she was called out on, but then none of them see her when she goes home.

It was a quiet night. They got a callout for an older woman who had chest pains, and that was the extent of their callouts all night.

Jessy and Mitch enjoyed the evening getting to know each other. They sat around the fireplace at the station, drinking hot chocolate. Jessy found it to be very relaxing. Perhaps it was because Mitch was three years older than her and had been doing this job longer than she had, where Ryan was just young and it was his first hitch. Ryan was a person who wouldn't sit. He was constantly pacing, and it made Jessy crazy.

Mitch, on the other hand, sat back with his feet up and chatted about some of the work he had done, but most of all, they talked about everything else. It was a relief to know someone else had a life besides being an EMT. Don't get her wrong, she loved her job, but there was more to life than that. Jessy loved to horseback and go canoeing even though she didn't do it as often as she would have liked. Nevertheless, she was game to have fun.

She found Mitch very interesting. He also loved horseback riding and canoeing. They thought perhaps one day they would do it together. Jessy always wanted to go white-water rafting, and Mitch thought that would be a blast. So they were thinking ahead of when they could go on this adventure together.

Jessy had found out that Mitch had been married right out of high school, and it lasted only a year. They were just kids and thought it would be cool to get married. They found out it wasn't so much fun after all and decided to go their own ways. They were glad they hadn't had a baby in that time. His wife had gone back to college as he had gone back to get his medical training. They still spoke now and again. The last time he heard from her, she was dating and she said they had talked about marriage, but she was afraid of it going the same way theirs had, and she was putting him off.

For Mitch, he never really dated again. He was happy just hanging out as friends. He said he had had one-night stands, but it was something they had both agreed on. So come morning, they went their separate ways, never having to worry about repercussions. Although one-night stands didn't feel right to him, he would fall for it now and again. He laughed to the excuse that, after all, he was a man and human, and sometimes, a warm body to snuggle close to gave him the jumpstart he needed to carry on.

Jessy sat in silence and studied him as he talked. She had learned that Mitch's mom had passed away a few years ago with cancer and his dad just went on doing his own thing. Mitch didn't talk like they were close, but he still respected his dad. She thought he was from Texas, and he was built like a football player. A very good-looking one at that.

Jessy liked that he was settled in a way that it wasn't all party and talk. That would drive her crazy when she would have to work with the men who had to talk about what they didn't get on the weekend. Oh, they talked, all right, but she knew they weren't as lucky as they liked her to believe. It wasn't changing her mind about dating them.

She didn't believe in mixing work with pleasure, not on a dating level. There were things she would do as friends, and that was all.

When their shift was over, she found she wasn't tired at all. It was an evening that she had enjoyed very much. It had been a long time since she had sat and talked with a man close to her own age. It actually felt good. Jessy felt alive.

"Jessy, would you like to go for coffee and a doughnut before you go home?"

"I don't think I need either, but sounds like a great idea."

"All right. I will meet you at Tim Horton's in ten minutes."

"Will do."

Jessy repacked her bag and got her things ready for her next shift. She knew Mitch had gone to have a shower. Most of the men shower before they went home. Jessy knew it was to get rid of any blood or any antiseptic that they might have gotten on them. Most of their wives or girlfriends were squeamish about it. She liked to wait and have her bath when she got home, usually with a book.

Mitch will have changed his clothes. Jessy will still be in uniform, but what did that matter? It wasn't a date.

She left and headed for the coffee shop. This time of day, it would be getting busy with the changing of shifts and so many others on their way to either work or home. She thought she should order so they would have a table, but not knowing what Mitch liked made it hard. After you work with each other for a while, you get to know each other's likes and dislikes and bad habits. You become a family away from home. Jessy figured that some of them were closer to each other than they were to their family members. That thought made her feel sad. She couldn't think of any one closer to her than her mom and dad.

She had a hard time when she would hear how some of her coworkers talked about their families. She always wondered what it would really be like to have a brother or a sister. Trisha was about as close as a sister could be, or at least Jessy thought so. Not having siblings, she didn't know what it really felt like, so she didn't judge those who talked badly of their family, but she always felt bad for them. She had always wished for siblings.

Her mom had told her that she had been too young to have children. They had had Jessy right out of high school, and Sharon had a miscarriage after Jessy. It was early in to the pregnancy, so they didn't even know what it was. They just never tried for any more. Then with her and Peter divorcing, more babies were out of the question.

Sharon never wanted babies with anyone else, and she took it that Peter was happy with just having Jessy. Many times Sharon felt guilty that Jessy never had siblings, but their lives went on without them. Just having Jessy gave Peter and Sharon a chance to see Jessy got all out of the educational programs that she could. Money was not an issue, not that they were rich, but Peter was very careful on how he spent his money. Jessy gave her mom and dad plenty of notice on how much her schooling was going to be costing, and that gave them time to save up. Jessy worked any kind of job she could get to help save for what she wanted, sometimes coming up with almost half of the amount. Having more children could have created a money problem.

When Mitch finally got to the coffee shop, he had ordered the same as Jessy, to which she thought, *That makes it simple while ordering from work or the drive-through.*

Jessy was surprised to see that they had sat and talked for another hour before finally going home. She had not realized they would find so much more to talk about, but they had.

Jessy went home feeling happy. She didn't know how to explain it but to say she was happy.

Jessy was an upbeat person most of the time, so for her to feel happy, it was on the inside. Jessy had never felt this way and was feeling silly about it. Shrugging, she just passed it off and went about her daily routine.

Putting on some music from the sixties' rock and roll made her housecleaning more fun. Lord knows Jessy didn't like housecleaning, but there came times when the dust bunnies were bigger then her slippers, and she was not sure whether to pick them up or stick her feet into them and use them for slippers. She knew if her mother saw that, she would be on her back like a raped ape.

When the day was over, Jessy stood back and took a long look at her little apartment, thinking, *Man, do I live a boring life, and my home shows it. Except now it's clean.*

Chapter 10

Since Mitch had become Jessy's partner, the days seemed to go by fast. They always had something to talk about, and having so many of the same interests, they could discuss matters big or small.

Jessy didn't know if it was the same for Mitch, but every time he was around her, she felt warm and happy inside. What did this mean to her? She had no idea. Jessy had thought about asking her mom, but then she knew her mom would make a big deal out of nothing. Not wanting to spoil the good feeling, she decided to keep it to herself.

The accidents they had to deal with didn't seem to be all that bad now that she was working with Mitch. Of course, a loss of life or someone badly hurt was always a horrible thing, Jessy finally felt at ease with her job. She felt it was because Mitch had confidence about himself and his ability to do his job right. Mitch covered all angles and never missed a beat. Jessy found this to be refreshing, and she liked the fact that she only had to worry about herself and her mistakes. Training someone on the job wasn't for Jessy.

Yes, she still double-checked everything. It was a good habit to keep. Not having to do the job for two people was easier on the nerves. Jessy felt that she had more time on her hands because Mitch was so efficient. Jessy found at the end of a full day she still had plenty of energy. Something she had been lacking. Jessy had been pushing herself to get done what had to be done in a day. Now it all came and went like she had no worries. Jessy had to admit she was loving the break and hoped it would go on for a long time.

Wednesday, Jessy was headed back out to the farm to work with Jumper, and Mitch was going with her. Mitch was impressed that Jessy had her veterinarian practice on the side and that she took it just as seriously as she did being a paramedic. To know this woman didn't sit at home on her days off and catch up on the soaps was amazing. Mitch didn't know many women who missed their afternoon shows.

Jessy had told Mitch about her dream and that she was working hard to see it come true. She wanted her own veterinary hospital. She wanted it to be big enough to sling a horse or two. Jessy knew of neighbors who shot their horses due to broken legs. She hoped she could put a stop to that.

Picking Mitch up at six thirty would give her the whole day with her dad. She missed her time spent with him. He was always full of interesting stories. She had wondered what she would do when the time came to say good-bye to her dad. Her mom was equally important to her, just in a different way. She knew that her life without them would be lonely, and it would be a whole new way of living. She also knew it was the way of life and the circle had begun so many years ago.

"Gosh, you believe in an early start on your days off?"

"You bet. I love spending time at the farm, so I go early. Dad is up before the sun, so we don't have to worry about waking him up."

"Oh, like daughter, like father."

"I guess you could say that. I always get a lot out of my time spent with my dad."

They were met at the drive as they pulled in by Peter with his gun in his hand.

"What the hell is this?" Mitch asked as he looked across at Jessy.

"I don't know," she said as she put her truck into park. They looked at each other then Mitch said, "Isn't this a bit soon? We haven't even dated, let alone slept together."

That had Jessy turning red and slapping Mitch on the arm. "Come. I'm sure there's a good reason for the gun."

"If you don't mind, I think I will stay right here."

"A coward, are you?"

"Yes, and I hope to be a live one when this day is over."

Jessy opened her door as Peter stood to the side. "Morning, Dad. Hunting early, aren't you"?

"I have a damn bear in the far pasture, tore up one of my calves."

Mitch, hearing that, got out of the truck and walked around to meet Peter.

"I will look at the calf, Dad."

"No need, Jessy. It's too late for the calf, but the bastard isn't getting another."

Jessy looked at her dad, like she was looking at a stranger. Peter never swore like that.

"Dad, this is my partner, Mitch Acorn."

Mitch, holding out his hand to Peter, was thinking today wasn't a good day to come and meet Jessy's dad. "It's a pleasure to meet you, sir."

"Same here," Peter said as he shook Mitch's hand, getting a surprise while doing so. He expected a soft hand and a limp wrist. Peter didn't have much use for men who didn't have a solid handshake. He always said they were not trustworthy. Jessy could see a slight grin come across his face as he said to Mitch, "Sorry, son. I don't usually greet people with a gun in my hands."

"I understand. Are you going hunting now for the bear?"

"Yes. I want to get it before it gets another calf. I'm just saddling up now."

"Would you mind if I joined you? I haven't had the opportunity to ride for quite some time."

"I would love the company. Jessy, you coming?"

"No, Dad. I want to work with Jumper. You two go ahead."

"Can you handle him alone, Jessy?" Mitch asked.

"Yes, thank you. Go with my dad and enjoy your ride."

The men saddled up, and Peter had gotten another gun for Mitch. "Do you know how to use this thing? Am I safe out there with you?"

"Yes, sir, I will watch your back."

"Okay, let's go. Jessy, we should be back by noon. We are going to the north side."

"Do you have your phone, Dad?"

"Yes, dear, right here." Peter patted his hip where his phone always hung.

"Check in from time to time. That way, I don't need to worry?"

"You don't need to worry anyways. I have my gun and backup today."

"So true. Just be careful." Jessy kissed her dad's cheek and hugged him. This stirred a warm feeling in Mitch, and he had to turn away. What would it be like to have someone love you like that?

"All right, son, let's go." Peter smacked his horse on the rump, and off he went.

"Talk to you soon, Jessy."

"Have a great ride, Mitch." She waved at him as he too slapped his horse on the rump and caught up to Peter.

The day was going by fast. The men had called home twice, and Peter said they had found another couple of dead calves and broken fence, which he figured the cows had run through getting away from the bear. They were going to repair the fence and bring the cows in with them and put them in a pasture closer to the house until he could find the bear.

"I'm going to ride up away and see if I can spot the bear. Did you want to start repairing the fence? I won't be long."

"I can do that, sir."

"Please, call me Peter, and there should be gloves, a hammer, and some staples in the pouch of the saddle. We don't ever leave home without them."

"Okay, I can handle that."

"Be careful. Keep your eyes in the back of your head."

Mitch had never heard that saying. "You too."

Peter had ridden probably two miles down when he came to the end of the bear tracking. Getting off his horse, he walked across the fence line to see if the tracks had headed into the bush, and sure enough, there were tracks along with blood. So the bear had carried a calf or part of a calf with it.

Peter took time to fix the fence there as well. While doing so, he thought that this bear must be a big brute. It sure the hell was hard on the fence. Once he was done fixing the fence, he rounded up what cattle were around, and he headed back to where Mitch was.

He had hoped this wasn't too much for the man to handle, although he seemed to be built like a football player, and he did look like he could handle whatever came his way. He also knew looks could be deceiving, and he also knew paramedics had to be tough to lift people. His daughter was not a big girl, but she had biceps on her and could lift her own weight. He knew Jessy could take care of herself, and yet she was a very pretty girl who was very much a woman. He loved to see her in dresses, which didn't happen often because of her work and the farm. Still, he knew he had a beautiful daughter. He always felt blessed that he had a beautiful wife, and she had given him another gift of beauty when she had had Jessy.

Yeah, Peter felt he had a lot to be happy for and proud of. Neither his wife nor daughter ever let him down nor caused him any hardships, even going through their divorce.

Sharon worried about Peter and what it would do to him. She had worked herself up to such a state over it, he had to calm her down. With that thought in his mind, it brought a smile to his face because the calming of Sharon had taken them to bed together, and he couldn't help but think at the time, if that was what divorcing was like, he was all for it although it didn't change the fact that they were still divorced. He knew deep in his heart at that moment Sharon would always be his woman and the love of his life.

Peter could relive so many of their times together that would put a smile on his face and make his days bearable. God, he missed Sharon, and he so wanted her back under his roof. Just how the hell was he going to do it and not spoil what they had? His thoughts were high on Sharon, and he knew she would be there tonight, wrapped in his arms in front of the fire as they sat and went over their week. He could still get aroused by just thinking of her and knowing that his love for her was stronger now than it was when they were younger. He shook his head, thinking, "Good God, man. You're not a teenager. Keep your mind on your work."

At that moment, he heard a scream. He didn't know where it came from, but he bet it was from Mitch. So he put his horse on full gallop and forgot about the cattle he was herding back.

Feeling the rip and the explosion of the pain had Mitch spinning around. He said, "What the hell!" just to be facing one of the biggest red bears he had ever seen. Their eyes met, and Mitch had always heard that if you keep eye contact, you can stare them down to where they will just leave. Holding on to his shoulder, he could feel the blood running over his hand, but he never tried to take a look. Being scared shitless was an easy way to just keep staring.

He whispered to himself, "Wow, aren't you a beauty!"

Just then he heard a gunshot, and the bear stood there and roared like he was taking on the world. Mitch thought, *Good God, am I going to die today?* just as the bear slapped him across the head. The gunshot caused them to lose eye contact. Mitch could feel the pain ripping through his head as he lay on the ground. He could feel the blood running and had no idea what had been cut. Now he was too weak from fear to try and get away. He was sure Peter had done the shooting. Again another gunshot was fired, and the bear fell right down on top of Mitch. He held his breath, which he thought was for a very long time, waiting for Peter.

Peter was lifting the bear's leg off so he could see Mitch's face, but all he could see was blood everywhere. Putting his hand on Mitch's chest to see if he was breathing, he asked, "Mitch, can you hear me, man?"

Peter had no way of knowing how bad Mitch was hurt or if he was bleeding to death.

Chapter 11

Mitch finally let out his breath and said, "It hurts like hell, Peter."

"Where, Mitch?"

"My right shoulder. The bear got my right shoulder."

"Your face too?"

"The side, yes."

"I'm calling Jessy. Hang in there."

Mitch was so dizzy he thought he would pass out. He fought it. He wanted to stay alert. He could hear Peter telling Jessy about the bear attack, and Mitch knew he would be in good hands in a few minutes.

"Hey, man, Jessy is on her way, and she was calling for backup. Hang in there, okay? I'll pull the bear off."

Things were going a little fuzzy, and Mitch tried to stay awake, but he knew he was losing the battle.

When Peter couldn't get Mitch to answer him anymore, he worked hard and fast, getting his horse tied to the bear to pull it off Mitch. Once he had Mitch freed of the bear, Peter looked Mitch over and took off his bandana from around his neck, trying to apply pressure where he saw it was bleeding the heaviest. He didn't think Mitch's wounds were all that bad, but then what the hell did he know? It looked like he would need some stitching up, for sure. There was no doubt about that.

Jessy was there sooner than Peter had thought she would be, and he was so relieved to see his daughter. Jessy would know what to do, and so he just stood back and watched and helped when needed. Like Sharon, he was taken by how Jessy just dove right in doing whatever had to be done.

The Stars ambulance was there within minutes of Jessy arriving, and before Peter knew it, Mitch was in the air.

"Dad, are you okay?" Jessy asked as she could see her dad's hands shaking and full of blood.

"Yes, I'm fine."

"Come, Dad. I will help you finish up here."

Peter rode back out and rounded up the cattle, and Jessy drove in behind him just to make sure there wasn't another bear on their trail. A beautiful day turned sour within minutes, and to think that we take each day for granted, and we all live with the idea *It won't happen to me.*

Jessy and Peter both cleaned up and headed into town to see how Mitch was doing. Jessy called her mom to tell her what had happened. Sharon had become shook up instantly, thinking it was Peter. Jessy finally got her to calm down and listen to what she was saying, or so she thought.

"Mom, meet us at the hospital, okay?"

"I'm on my way, Jessy." She dropped the phone and ran for her car. Sharon's heart was pounding so hard she thought she would pass out. "Calm down, Sharon, Peter is fine." Sharon kept saying this over and over in her head, but she knew nothing would do the trick until she saw Peter for herself.

Her hands shook so much she couldn't get the key into the ignition. Sharon put her head down onto the steering wheel, and taking a couple of deep breaths, she waited until she could move her hand with control.

Sharon got to the hospital just as Peter and Jessy were pulling in. Tears came to her eyes as she pulled to a stop and worked on her seatbelt to get freed. As she opened the door, Peter was there to take her hand and help her out.

"Oh, Peter," was all she could say as he pulled her in for a hug. She sobbed on his shoulder.

"Now, now, Sharon. I'm fine, and so is Jessy. You worry too much, sweetheart. Look, Sharon, I'm in one piece, and so is Mitch. He will need some stitching, but I'm sure he will be just fine. He may have a beauty of a scar to brag about and tell his children and grandkids, but all in all, I think he will be as good as new."

"It could have been you, Peter."

"Yes, dear, it could have been, but it's not, and I'm standing here with you." He pulled her in closer and kissed the top of her head before saying, "Now let's go up and find Jessy and Mitch."

"Oh my god, of course. Jessy must be worried out of her mind for Mitch."

"Our daughter holds it together remarkably well."

"Yes, she does."

"We were lucky to have her at the farm today. She called Stars. Something I would never have thought of. I would have just put Mitch in the truck and drove him into town. It would have been much harder on him and a lot longer.

Within minutes, they had him in the air. Mind you, Jessy had him ready to go by the time they landed."

"It's a good thing you have open fields, hey."

"Oh, for sure." Getting off the elevator, they saw Jessy standing at the desk. They walked over to stand behind her to hear what was going on.

"How long will he be under?"

"He will be back in recovery, if all goes as planned in couple hours."

"Okay, thank you."

"What is going on, Jess?" Peter asked.

"They are going to repair Mitch's shoulder. The bear tore it apart pretty good. So they are hoping with the specialist that is on his way. They should be able to save it. He will be laid up for a while."

"Gosh, I hope they can save it. He depends on that shoulder for a lot."

"Yes, Mom. It is one of the main parts of our body we need for our jobs. It sucks that I will have to have a new partner at work again."

"I don't think he will be kept down long. He doesn't seem to be a sort of man that would like to lie around."

"That's true, Dad. Mitch likes to be busy all the time."

"Oh, a man after your own heart," he said as he winked at her. Peter knew Jess had no use for lazy people. Many times he had told her that some people need to take breaks and couldn't work like she did. Her reply was always the same: Do your job then take a break for as long as you want.

"I want to go see Mitch before he goes for surgery."

"Do you mind if we come and see him as well?"

"Of course not. I think that he would like that."

With that said, they all went to see Mitch. He was lying with his eyes closed. No doubt they had given him something stronger for the pain that would make him drowsy.

Jessy went over to the side of his bed and placed her hand on his arm. Mitch opened his one eye as the other one had swollen and changed color already. He got a faint smile across his face as he said, "Hey, partner."

"How you feeling, Mitch?"

"Higher than a kite right now."

"That's good. Are you in pain?"

"No, Jess. I don't feel a damn thing right now."

"Mom and Dad came to see you too." She stepped aside so her parents could step up and talk to Mitch.

Mitch held out his hand for Peter to take, and when Peter took hold of it, he knew this football player wasn't going out without a fight. He may be weak, but he still had strength in his hand. They did not get around to a shake, but they held hands for a moment, and neither one of the men seem bothered by it.

"Let us know if there is anything we can do for you, son. I'm sorry this happened to you."

"Aw, don't be. It wasn't your fault."

"I should not have left you alone when I knew a bear was wandering around there. Who leaves someone alone like that? It was totally stupid on my part."

"I had a gun."

"A lot of good that did you."

"You told me to use the eyes in the back of my head."

"You told him that, Peter?" Sharon asked.

"Yes, Sharon. Out there, you have to or—"

"This happens," Mitch said.

"I thought it was just mothers who had eyes in the back of their heads."

"No, Sharon. It's because you women think you are the only ones who can see back there." They all laughed with that, and then Peter said, "Do you girls want to go eat?"

"I'm not hungry, Dad. You and Mom go. I will visit with Mitch until they come for him."

Just at that moment, a nurse came in. "That won't be long. The specialist is here and going over everything, so we have to make sure you're going to be ready when they call."

"All right, Mitch. Good luck, and Sharon and I will come see you after they fix you up."

"Thank you." Mitch let go of Peter's hand and watched them leave as Jessy moved back in closer to the bed.

"You know, you are a sight for sore eyes."

Jessy blushed and said, "You mean sore eye."

Mitch nodded. "I'm glad you were close by, Jessy. I was scared to death when that bear was on top of me. After Peter shot him, all I could think was, 'Jessy, please get here.' I was so afraid of passing out and no one knowing where I was. Good God, Jessy, did you see the size of him? I have never seen anything like it."

Mitch's words were a little slow in coming out and some were slurred, but Jessy could still understand what he said. She hung on to every word he said.

"Yes, Mitch. I took pictures of him with my phone camera so you can show the guys at work. They will see they don't want to mess around with you."

Mitch nodded but had a hard time keeping his eyes open.

"You sleep if you want. I'm not going anywhere."

Mitch got a grin on his face but didn't reply.

Jessy pulled up a chair and went through her contacts to let people at work know that Mitch was in the hospital and she would be in soon to explain and for them not to come up to the hospital yet. She would sit and wait until they took him away.

Sitting and looking at him, she thought, *What a gorgeous man, even with a torn-up face.*

When they finally took Mitch to surgery, Jessy went down to the station as she had said she would. The reaction of their workmates was mixed from disbelief to despair. The concern for the new man in their unit touched Jessy. By the time she was headed back up to see Mitch, they had gotten a card, and everyone had signed it for him. After all, they were now his family.

Mitch was still very groggy. He knew she was there but couldn't stay awake, and she knew this would happen, so she stayed with him. She watched as the nurses came in and checked his vitals, and they would chat away at Mitch. Sometimes he answered, and other times he just grunted. That made her chuckle to herself. To see such a big man out of control was priceless. It was like watching a drunk. Then she wondered what he would be like drunk. Jessy figured he would be a happy, fun drunk.

After the nurses left them alone, Mitch wanted a drink, so Jessy helped him.

"Remember to go slow or you will throw up, and I don't want to be cleaning that up, thank you."

Mitch nodded as he took a drink. "Thank you for being here, Jess."

"You're welcome. There is no need to thank me. We are partners, remember?"

"Yeah, I remember. Looks like I'm going to be laid up awhile."

"It looks like I will be getting a new partner. If you wanted out, all you had to do was say so. You didn't have to tackle a bear, for Pete's sake."

"Now's a fine time to tell me that, Jess."

She chuckled as she fixed the blanket on the bed. They had a very easy relationship, and they liked to tease each other. It made working together more fun, and it was always an interesting day whenever she was with Mitch. She was going to miss him at work. She knew she would visit him once he got home, but it wouldn't be the same as working together.

With how hospitals are run today, Mitch was sent home the next afternoon. They said he was so healthy he wouldn't have any problems and should heal fast.

As always, you can't wait to get home, but once at home, you wonder why you didn't ask to stay just one more day. Mitch had called a cab to take him home and was thinking he should call one to take him back to the hospital when Jessy showed up at his door.

"What the hell are you doing? Why didn't you call me?" she said as she grabbed him by the arm as he stumbled toward the sofa.

"Nice to see you too."

"I'm sorry, but you should have called. I thought you would be in for a few days. I had things to do before I came up to see you. I was surprised to hear they sent you home."

"Don't worry so much, Jessy. I will be fine."

"I can see that."

"Well, maybe in a bit. Right now, I feel like I have to throw up."

"Just wait on that." Jessy ran and got the garbage can.

"I feel like shit, Jess."

"You don't look so good right now either. Here, lie down. May I get you a pillow from your bedroom?"

"Yes, thanks."

While she was doing that, she was noticing how neat yet manly it was in his place. There was no sign of any woman's touch. She had been as far as his kitchen, and even that, now that she thought about it, was neat. That was all she could use to describe it.

"Here now. Maybe you will feel better if you just lie still for a while." She put the blanket that was folded over the chair over him.

"Did they know you were going to be alone when you came home?"

"They never asked, so when the papers were all signed, I called a cab."

Mitch wasn't down for too long before he fell asleep. Jessy took that time to go into his kitchen to see what she could find to make for him to eat. Lipton's chicken noodle soup—just what the doctor ordered. She had it on simmer when he finally woke up.

"This tastes better than I remember it tasting."

"It always does when you're not feeling good and when someone else makes it."

"You have a point. You don't have to stay, Jess. I know you have things to tend too at the farm," Mitch said as he tried to get up.

"Where you going?"

"To the bathroom, Jess. That's all."

"Here let me help you."

"To the bathroom?"

"Yes, to the bathroom."

He looked at her like she had lost her mind.

"Mitch, I will help you to the bathroom door then you are on your own. Unless you fall or something."

"Okay. I haven't had anyone take care of me for a long time. I think I was ten when I had my tonsils out, and that was a very long time ago."

"Well, don't get used to it, buddy. Just a couple days until you get all the drugs out of your system."

"Jess, you don't have to stay."

"I know that, and I won't. I will pop in and out just to make sure you're eating and that you're not overdoing the shoulder because I want you back to work."

"That's nice of you. Thank you." With that, Mitch fell back to sleep.

Jessy sat in his big overstuffed chair, and she also fell asleep. She woke to Mitch's cursing as he tried to get up.

"Hey, let me help you."

"Sorry. I didn't mean to wake you."

"No worries. That's why I'm here to help."

"Did you go home at all?"

"No, I fell asleep, I'm sorry to say."

"Don't be sorry. Hope you slept well."

"Surprisingly, I did. How about you?"

"A little pain, but nothing I can't handle. But I do need a painkiller now."

"Are you going to shower first?"

"Can't shower yet. They told me two days then shower. I can sit in the bath, which might be nice. Would help relax back muscles."

"Okay. Call if you need help."

Raising an eyebrow, he looked at her and said, "Are you serious?"

"Yes, I am. That's why I'm here."

"So you will help me how?"

"Whatever you need help with."

With a frown, he said, "So seeing how I can't wash my back, would that be asking too much?"

Jessy didn't even hesitate. "Not at all. I would think that would be a little hard to do the way they have you wrapped up."

Grinning, Mitch said, "Deal. I will call you when I'm ready." He headed for the bathroom.

Jessy went to the kitchen sink and washed her face and hands, and then she looked around to see what he had on hand for coffee. She wasn't finding anything, so she was making a trip to Timmy's. *Can't start a day without coffee.*

"Hey, Mitch,"

"Yeah, Jess."

"I'm running down to Timmy's to grab us coffee. Will you be okay for a few?"

"You bet. Thank you, that sounds great."

"Okay, be back shortly."

"I will still be here."

Jessy chuckled to herself as she left Mitch soaking in the tub.

Mitch leaned back and smiled. It had been a long time since he has had a girl in his home, and having one who was actually doing something nice for him—well, how much better could it get?

"Hi, Jessy. How is Mitch today?"

"Hi, Dad! Mitch is a little stiff. He is soaking in the tub, so I came to get us some coffee. What are you doing in town so early? Something wrong?"

"No, nothing wrong. Just thought I would check on Mitch."

"You going to come over then?"

"Later. I'm going to go take your mom out for breakfast."

"Aw, that's sweet of you."

"She doesn't know that. I'm surprising her."

"I think you should have given her time to get ready."

"Your mom is always ready. She has always made that a priority thing for herself."

"Going out for breakfast, she might want to be a little more picky about what she looks like."

"Oh well, guess I will have to wait."

They both laughed. Peter hugged Jessy, and they parted ways. Jessy noticed her dad was going into the flower shop. It warmed her heart to see he was thinking that way of her mother.

Jessy hurried and got their coffees, and she also grabbed them some tea biscuits. "Hey, Mitch, I'm back."

"Just in time. If you could do my back, I'm ready to get out."

"Be right there." Jessy put their breakfast on the table and went in to wash Mitch's back.

"Oh my god," was all she could say when she saw his back.

"What is it, Jess?" Mitch now had fear in his voice.

"No wonder your back aches, Mitch. You are so swollen, and there isn't a white piece of skin anywhere."

"Well, I am dark skinned, you know."

"No, you're all colors, and skin isn't one of them." She took the cloth and gently washed his back.

Although Mitch could feel it, he knew that she was being as gentle as could be. It hurt more than it felt good, but he wanted the hospital smell gone, so he would put up with the discomfort.

"Boy I think they drowned you with that disinfectant that they use. That alone will take a while to wash off."

"It's the smell I don't like."

"Okay, you're done back here."

"My bath towel is behind the door."

Jessy got his bath towel and held it up so he could get up and wrap himself up into it.

"You good to go now?"

"Yes, Jessy, thank you."

"No problem." Jessy left the bathroom and got their biscuits on to their plates and had their coffee waiting when Mitch came out.

"Sorry, Jess. I couldn't do the pants-and-shirt thing, so my house coat will have to do."

"I'm sorry. I never thought about that."

"Getting out of them was one thing with one hand, but getting into them was a problem."

"I can imagine. Come sit and have your coffee and breakfast."

"Breakfast too?"

"It's not much. I didn't know how much you dare eat yet, or would it make you sick?"

"Good thinking. I like their biscuits, so it will do for now. Thank you."

"I saw Dad in town. He said he would come over later. He was taking Mom out for breakfast."

"Do they spend a lot of time together?"

"Yes, they do."

"So why don't they live together?"

"'Cause they are divorced."

"They are? I thought they were just separated."

"They have been divorced for years."

"But they seem to really care for each other."

"Oh, they do. I don't know what is holding them apart. I'm just glad that they do have the relationship that they do have. Sure makes it easier on me. At first it was tough, just because I didn't know what they wanted to do, but it soon fell into place, and we have all been happy this way."

"Strange."

"You're telling me. I had always hoped that they would get back together."

"They're not really apart, are they?"

"Guess not in the same way as others that are divorced."

"Maybe someday they will move back in together."

"I don't know. They're both happy this way and set in their ways now."

"I guess whatever works, hey."

"Yeah. I get to spend lots of time with them both at the farm, so that's fine with me. They never put me in the middle of anything. They always have put me first, and I had worried at first if that was what split them up. But they both say no. They were just too young."

"Well, I know firsthand that happens."

As promised, Peter did go see Mitch. By this time, Jessy had gone home to do things she had to tend to but told Mitch she would be back. He never doubted it for a moment.

Peter had told him that he had brought the bear in to be stuffed, and he wanted it to be put into their museum. He couldn't just leave him in the bush. The great red bear had a history, and he was part of that community. The bear had been the talk of their community for years, and he was still the talk. So Peter felt that it was only right to have him displayed where the people he haunted could now go and see the ghost bear.

It was something they could tell their children and grandchildren about for years to come. He had asked the staff at the museum to collect stories on the bear and display them as well. They were going to put an ad in the paper asking for stories to be brought in.

Peter had told them his story and how the bear had finally been killed. Up until he attacked Mitch, the ghost bear had hurt no one. He also told them that it was the biggest red bear he had ever seen. Hell, it was the biggest bear he had ever seen, period. There were stories for years about this bear. So many people talked about him, but not many saw him. It saddened Peter to know he was the one who had ended the bear's life and his legacy.

Chapter 12

Jessy had combined work with helping Mitch. Her days were full, and she loved every minute of it. She never complained. She felt more alive now than she had for a very long time. Until now, she didn't realize that she had been in a slump. All this time she thought life was great and she was happy doing what she wanted to do and it was something she was good at.

Mitch had given her the lift that she hadn't known she needed.

Jessy's new partner was Emily Becon. She was eight years older than Jessy and very wise and great on the job. Jessy figured if Emily was around long enough, she might learn some new tricks of the trade from her. Emily was married, and her husband was a millwright. They had four children and a busy life. Emily never had a free moment, and she too seemed to thrive on it.

When Jessy found out that Emily has been doing this right out of school and took time off just to have her babies and she made it all work—marriage, a family, and this job—she just shook her head, asking, "How do you do it?"

Everyone else Jessy worked with complained about their home life and how they didn't have one. Emily was living proof that you could have both and be happy. This made Jessy take a deep breath and smile to herself.

A blissful life was what she wanted, and she was learning that it wasn't by being alone.

Emily only filled in when needed. So when Mitch came back, Emily would stay at home with her family until they needed her again.

Mitch healed fast. He had gotten an infection, but they hit him hard with treatment. He had taken his rehab seriously and was back to work before he was missed too much by some people. Jessy missed him right from the start. She was glad that they were friends enough that she could be with him after work and help him out.

The day Mitch came back to work, Jessy had booked an appointment for a lube job. Their unit was in need of one, and with all the drive-throughs they wouldn't be tied up long.

They were looking over some of the new machines that were in the showroom while waiting. They had just been told their unit was ready when all hell broke loose. Police sirens were going, and fire trucks went flying by.

"We better see what's up," Mitch said as they walked by this tall young man who seemed to be about seventeen and totally baffled. Then they heard him say, "Are you for real?"

The young man turned white, and Mitch stepped over to him, asking, "Hey, man, are you okay?"

"My truck just killed someone."

"What?"

ROAD SIDE CROSSES

"The dealer from here took my truck for a test drive and was in an accident with it. They said a man was killed."

Jessy and Mitch looked at each other as if to say they didn't believe him.

"We better get going," Jessy said.

"Sorry, man. Hope all works out."

Mitch and Jessy ran for their unit. As they opened the doors, they heard their call come in. It was just a couple of blocks from where they were at, on the main highway west bound. When they arrived on the scene, it was unbelievable. A car with a single passenger in it had come down the one way the wrong way, wiping out the truck.

He was pronounced dead at the scene, and the driver in the truck would need Jaws of Life to get him out. What a mess. You could not tell what kind of car it was. The truck was a heavy diesel but had no front wheels left on it, and it was a twisted mess. There was a big man in the driver's seat.

The highway was closed and traffic rerouted for four hours. Mitch and Jessy helped get the dead man into an ambulance. He looked like he was in his early sixties, but it was hard to tell. It was just a wild guess. The smell of booze was heavily laden in the car, so it was probably the main factor in the accident.

They had learned what the young man had said was the truth. He had taken his truck in to see what he could get for a trade-in. What a shocker for someone so young.

The police said they had gotten a couple of calls on a car traveling down the wrong lane at a fast speed. They had hoped they would get to him first. There was talk of suicide. Who would ever know? No one knew what was going on with the man or what was going through his mind at the time, so people had to think of a reason. Suicide was their answer.

The truck pulled out to pass a highboy, not expecting someone to be right there in his lane. There was no time to react. It was all over in minutes.

The family of the dead man were in shock. They were all so worried about the other driver. Was he going to live or die? He had gotten a broken back along with all the other injuries. It would take him a long time to recover if he ever did.

This was the first time Mitch had ever put a cross up on the side of the road. He could read Jessy's face, and he knew it was something she felt she had to do.

This was an experience that Mitch would never forget and one of many he would be involved in with Jessy. As she was placing the cross into the ground, she turned to Mitch and said, "You know, Mitch, from the moment you quit breathing, your sprit leaves your body. A graveyard is just a front and a moneymaker. There should be no charge to lay someone to rest. These souls have paid taxes their whole life. So they have earned a resting place here on earth while their spirit has earned a place in heaven. The poor people are facing the loss of a loved one, and some of them end up in debt because of it. To rob people at such a sad time in their lives is unbelievable. This is something that people should fight to change."

When she explained how she felt and what it meant to her, he could see the pain that Jessy felt for all her victims.

Jessy had shown Mitch her book of poems that she had written for all the victims she had dealt with. He was surprised by the amount of pictures she had also collected. She would mount their picture on the bottom of their page.

"How do you get their pictures, Jessy?"

"When I'm lucky enough to talk to the families, they usually don't mind sharing a picture of the one they have just lost."

"You sure have a way with people, Jess. This was your calling for sure." Mitch couldn't believe the compassion this woman had for strangers. It made him warm inside to know her. "I hope you will be there for me, Jessy, and be the one to write my final poem and put up my cross with feeling." He pulled her in for a bear hug.

"I hope I never have to do that for you or anyone else that I love." She laid her head on his chest.

Mitch thought it was time to lighten the mood. "Are you up for a Timmy's?"

"You bet I am."

"I buy this time."

"Okay." Mitch knew that Jessy liked to keep things square between them. She would never want anyone to think or feel she didn't pay her way or pull her own weight. Mitch had bought their morning coffee.

While sitting over their coffee, Mitch smiled at her and said, "You know, Jessy, we should buy one of these."

"One of what?"

"Timmy's. We almost live here."

She looked at him and said, "You're right, we do. Why do you think that is?"

"'Cause neither of us like to make coffee at home. This is quicker, and we leave the mess behind."

"Yeah, I like that part," Jessy said, and they laugh together. This was something they did a lot together and enjoyed.

Mitch enjoyed all the time they spent together, and so did Jessy. On their days off, they were at the farm and always found something to do.

It had gotten to be that Sharon and Peter expected Mitch to be with Jessy whenever they saw her. They had become a couple, and they didn't even know it. To everyone else it was obvious, but Jessy and Mitch never clued in. Their partnership had carried far beyond work, and it happened so smoothly no one made a big deal of it.

"Will you two be staying for supper?"

"Yes, Dad. We want to work with Jumper after we take his cast off. Why? Is there a problem?"

"No. Mom is coming out, and she said she wasn't up to cooking and she was bringing pizza. She just needed to know how much."

"Mom sick?"

"I'm not sure."

"Oh, that's not like her."

"No. Guess everyone has a down day, even your mother."

"Call us when she gets here."

"Will do."

Jessy and Mitch headed over to the barn where Jumper was. It was the day she had been waiting for. Jumper can have his cast taken off, and Jessy was excited to see how he would react. They had used a water hose with warm water to soak it off. The saw would have spooked him too much and perhaps caused injuries again.

Jessy could hear Mitch talking but never answered him too much. In fact, she was too quiet, even dealing with the horse. This drove Mitch crazy. This wasn't the Jessy he had come to know.

He went over to her and took her by the arm until she finally looked up at him with a confused look on her face.

"Is there a problem, Mitch?"

"I don't know. You tell me, Jessy. Have I said or done something to upset you?"

"No," she said with a frown, almost agitated.

"Then what's up? You're not talking, and you act like you're a million miles away."

"I'm sorry." She walked over to a five-gallon bucket that was sitting there and turned it over to sit on. "It's Mom."

"Your mom!" Mitch asked, surprised.

"Yeah." Jessy frowned.

"Come on, Jessy, what's up with your mom?"

"That's just it, I don't know."

"You don't know what?"

"Mom isn't cooking supper tonight."

"That's it? Your mom isn't cooking supper, and it has you like this?"

"Mitch, you have been around now long enough to know Mom. When has she come to the farm and not made us supper?"

"Never since I've known you."

"Exactly. She said she wasn't up to it. Something is wrong."

"Maybe she is really tired. She goes and goes like you. The apple doesn't fall far from the tree. Remember, she is older than you. Give the woman a break."

"Yeah, true. Maybe you're right."

"Well, don't go fretting about nothing."

"I suppose you're right." Yet Jessy wasn't completely convinced that all was well with her mother. So deep down inside, she would worry until she knew different.

When Sharon showed up, she was looking tired and she was quiet. Jessy was on alert. She knew there was something wrong even if her dad and Mitch didn't. They sat around eating their pizza and having a pleasant chitchat.

Jessy couldn't take it anymore. She reached over and put her hand on Sharon's arm. "What's wrong, Mom? You're so quiet."

"Nothing, dear. Guess I'm just tired. I have put in some long nights."

"You do that all the time, Mom. So why is it so different now?"

"I think my age is catching up to me, dear." Sharon laughed lightly.

All this time, Peter was watching her. He knew Sharon, and he also knew something was wrong.

Chapter 13

After supper, they all sat around the fireplace, chatting about the local events that had happened. Mitch and Jessy told them about the young man and the bizarre event in how his truck had been taken out for a test drive at the dealership and was totaled off by a man traveling down the one way the wrong way, killing himself and seriously injuring the driver of the truck. The fact that everyone was speculating on was suicide. No one will ever know the real truth.

"On a good note, I'm happy with how well Jumper has come along, and I'm looking forward to riding him again."

"He will be as good as new, Dad."

"Well, I won't use him like I used to, that's for sure. After all, he's not a young horse anymore."

"That's true, Dad, but don't be too easy on him because you won't help him build his strength up to what it should be. He has to be worked now to rebuild what he had before he broke his leg."

"I will ride him, Jessy, but I won't work him like I used to. It's time to semiretire him, anyway."

"You think we should do that to you too, Dad?"

They all laughed, except Sharon. She had sat listening to them chatting, but she hadn't said a word all night. When she did, it was just to say, "If you will all excuse me, I'm tired and going to turn in now."

"Okay, Mom, talk to you in the morning."

Sharon leaned over and kissed Jessy on the cheek. Then she turned and walked away. Jessy just carried on chatting with Mitch.

Peter had glanced at his watch and noticed it wasn't late at all. This wasn't the Sharon that he knew and loved. Peter sat around for about half an hour longer, and it was driving him crazy. He finally excused himself and went on up to bed. Once he had showered and climbed into bed, he tossed and turned. He kept thinking about Sharon and how quiet she had been. Not just tonight, but the last few times he had gone into town and took her out for meals. At first he put it off on what she had gone through on their trip to see Trisha. But that had been a while ago, and Sharon still wasn't herself.

This is bull. Something is wrong. He tossed his covers to the side and went down to Sharon's room. Opening the door quietly and slipping inside, he found her sitting in the big chair in front of the window. Going over, he placed his hands upon her shoulders. Not looking up at Peter, Sharon brought her hands up and put them down over his.

"You want to talk about it?" He still hadn't seen the tears that were slowly sliding down Sharon's cheeks.

Sharon sat quietly for a few more minutes before she pulled a Kleenex from her pocket. At that moment, Peter knew she had been crying, so he went around and knelt in front of her.

"What is it, babe? Please talk to me."

"Oh, Peter, it's nothing, really."

Raising his eyebrows, he said, "Sharon, it has you sitting in the dark alone, crying. So please don't tell me it's nothing. You have been so quiet and so far away now for some time. Have I done something to upset you? Do you not want to be here with us?"

With that said, Sharon started to cry again.

"Aw, babe, you don't have to come out and stay on weekends. I thought you were doing it because this is what you wanted to do, but if it's making you so sad, don't do it." He sat back on his heels, still holding her hands. Looking at her, he thought maybe he had best let go of her hands. So he slowly slid his hands from hers.

Sharon then saw the hurt in his eyes. That wasn't what she wanted to do. Hurting Peter had never crossed her mind.

"Oh, darling, no," she said as she reached for his hands again. "You know my heart will always be here. This is where it belongs and will stay till my dying day."

Now Peter was so damn confused he wanted to yell at her, *"Then what the hell has you acting this way?"* He held back because he knew Sharon well enough to know that it was something deep. Sharon never did anything without thinking it over well. He always felt she took too long sometimes in her decisions. He had also learned not to push because she never told until she was sure and ready.

How was she going to tell him she had made a mistake, the biggest mistake of her life? That alone will hurt him. To tell him she had changed her mind and wanted to come home was more than she could say. Oh, God, she loved this man, and all she wanted to do now was to be his wife. After all these years, she no longer wanted to work. Sharon wanted to be at the farm taking care of the only man she had ever loved. How was she going to tell him that when she was the one who asked for the divorce in the first place? Yes, they married too young and had a child, but now they are older and had grown into very mature adults with plenty of history behind them.

Now Sharon wanted to move on and plan a future with him. She no longer wanted to be alone at nights. Nor did she want to be alone when she awoke in the morning. Watching Peter go through his routine on weekends was like she had never left. But she had, and he had learned to live without her. Coming back would be upsetting the apple cart this late in their lives and could be more damaging than good. She knew he still had some kind of feelings for her, but was it enough for her to come back? Could she ever come home and be his wife again?

What about Jessy? How would she do with all of this? Jessy too had moved on and was happy in her life. Sharon knows Jessy would want her to promise to stay forever. Yet everyone knows forever is a long time, and what if her dreams of them living happily was just that, a dream? If they couldn't get on track and things didn't work out, what then? Would hearts be broken to the point that they wouldn't have what they have now living as they do? Would the two people who mean the most to her forgive her if she caused unnecessary pain? Would they continue to love her on some level as they do now? Or would they finally close the door on her and say enough was enough?

This made Sharon sick to the stomach just to think that if she screwed up, she would have lost her family. So no, it wasn't worth the risk. She would leave things as is.

"Just hold me, Peter, like you always do."

He stood up and pulled her up into his embrace. "Well, that I can do." He went to place a kiss on the top of her head just as she looked up, and so their lips met. It was a slow meaningful kiss that turned to hot passion within minutes. This had Peter picking Sharon up and taking her to her bed.

Their lovemaking always felt so right between them, and he could never think of himself with anyone else in his arms in an intimate way. God, he longed for her at nights when she was gone home. Some days his longing was so strong it made him uncomfortable. To love someone as he loved Sharon yet having to live under different roofs just didn't make any sense at all. What he wouldn't give if he could only talk Sharon into coming home.

To take the chance of losing what they have made him hold back asking. He had gone into Sharon many times in the last month to do just that. Scared of jeopardizing what they have now always made the words stay on the tip of his tongue.

How could he have been so foolish and gone along with the divorce in the first place was more then he could comprehend. Any man to love someone as deeply as he loved Sharon should have had his head examined when a divorce was mentioned. At the time he went along with it, it did seem right at the time and they have all lived very happily and a full life to this point. Why would he want to rock the boat? Why would he want to take a chance at messing up what he had now?

What about Jessy? She had learned to live with the way her parents live and had asked nothing of them.

Peter and Sharon never fought in front of her, nor did they ever put her in the middle of their disagreements. When he thought about it, disagreements were all they had. To say they fought wasn't true. As he laid there holding the love of his life in his arms and listening to her breathing so lightly and peacefully, he thought to himself, *Just what the hell did we divorce for?* It had been so many years he couldn't remember what it was over, but it had worked for them.

Yes, it took some time for them all to adjust, but in a short time, they just moved on and everything has been great. Then he thought, *Bullshit. I love my wife, and I miss her in my home with me every day.*

Closing his eyes, he says a silent prayer. *"Oh, Father, if you can hear me now. I am asking you for this one favor. Would you please help me find a way to ask my wife to come home? You know that she is always in my heart and always has been. I'm sure it's because of you that we are still a half-ass couple. Please, can you help me make us whole again without losing what we already have?"*

Sharon stirring brought Peter back into the present. He just wrapped his arms around her tighter as she snuggled in closer. He laid there looking at her as the light of the moon shone down on them. His wife had gotten prettier as the years had gone on. He thought it was funny how that worked with some people. To him, he had just gotten older, but not Sharon. She had aged very well. She was still someone to be proud to have on your arm. She would be a beautiful grandmother someday. With that thought in mind, Peter finally fell asleep.

His dreams were of him and Sharon as grandparents. He didn't know where all the kids had come from, but everyone was happy. He remembered looking across the picnic blanket at Sharon, and she was in seventh heaven holding a baby in her arms and having another one climbing on to her lap.

The dream ended abruptly as his alarm went off on his watch. "Shit." He rolled over and, picking it up off the nightstand, shut it off. He went back to sleep in hopes of picking up the dream where he had left off.

He finally woke up to Sharon bringing him breakfast in bed, like she used to. He couldn't remember the dream past the part that he had been woken from.

They had breakfast in bed, and their lovemaking then was just as loving as it had been the night before.

This made Peter want to ask her to come home. Once again, the fear of losing what they now shared made him keep his thoughts and wants to himself.

Sharon knew it would only make her sadder when she went home. She knew she was leaving the best thing that had ever been in her life behind, and she also knew that stupidity was standing in her way of having what all she wanted. To think of how many couples end up divorced, and they shouldn't have made her cry inside for all those broken hearts. She and Peter were a prime example of a couple who divorced and should have just gotten some help. Help, yes, that was what she needed now to fix what she had broken. But can it be done now after all these years?

"Hey, babe, you think we should get up and make fresh coffee for the kids before they get up?"

"Oh, Peter, they have been up for a long time already."

"They're young. They should still be in bed. We are the ones who should be up."

"It's our daughter you are talking about."

"Good point. Poor Mitch."

Chapter 14

"Oh, I don't think you have to worry about Mitch. He seems to be able to keep up to our daughter without a problem."

"Yeah, they do seem to be well matched, don't they?"

Raising an eyebrow, Sharon glanced up at Peter.

"What? Don't tell me you haven't thought of the two of them getting together."

"I have, but I also remember the speech you gave me about not pushing her into something that I wanted for her. To let her live her own life."

"Hey, who's pushing? I just said they were well matched."

"I don't think our baby girl will settle down so long as she keeps working. She has made that pretty plan to us over the years that her work is her life."

"Yes, she has. We can only dream."

"My, my, is someone getting a little anxious for grandchildren?"

"Well, you know we aren't getting any younger."

"Really." was all Sharon would say. This was a different side of Peter she had not seen before. When it was her talking this way, he had told her she was being selfish and just wanted grandkids and that she wasn't being fair to Jessy. To leave Jessy alone and let her live her own life. It had Sharon smiling to herself knowing she and Peter were now on the same page about their daughter.

"Well then, my dear, would you like to go for a horseback ride before you go home?" Those words stuck in his craw as she was home—she just didn't know it.

"I think that would be a grand idea. I haven't been riding for a very long time. It could prove to be interesting as well as painful."

"I know, and it's time you got back in the saddle, my dear, before you forget how to ride."

"Not a chance of that. It's like riding a bike. You never forget."

"Okay, you may not forget, but it will make you stiff and sore. You know, I have the perfect remedy to help with the stiffness and pain." He pulled her in for a hug and gave her a kiss on the forehead.

"That I believe." Sharon pat him on the chest as she backed away.

Peter and Sharon went riding for the rest of the morning. It was something they had done often when they were first together, and after Jessy was born, Sharon didn't go as often. Once in a while, she would put Jessy in her snuggle bag and take her along. Sharon didn't feel comfortable doing that in case the horse acted up. It was one thing for her to deal with the horse but not with a child on her back. Peter never understood the way she felt because he had total trust in his horses. Yet he never took Jessy with him. Sharon's riding days had been limited and far apart.

As they rode, much of their time was in silence. Both were thinking their own thoughts of what was and what had been. Neither wanted to say it to the other. They thought so much alike it was unreal, yet not sharing was keeping them apart.

Sharon caught Peter looking at her. She waited, but he didn't say a word.

"So what are you thinking, Peter? I see the wheels going around in that handsome head of yours, but you're not saying much."

"Oh, I was thinking of the days past, and how sweet they were."

"You mean our riding days?"

"Yes, them and other days as well. We did have plenty of great days, Sharon."

"I know, Peter. I will always be grateful for those days."

"We should do this more often."

"I agree."

"You do?"

"Yes, I do. I don't have to worry about bringing a baby along, so it is easier for me now. I am able to enjoy it more."

"You didn't enjoy the rides before?" Peter said with a frown.

"It's not that I didn't enjoy them. Having Jessy with me made me very nervous."

"You didn't have to be. You were always on Camilla, and she would never had harmed you."

"Sorry, Peter, but I was never as confident as you about that. Anything could have happened."

"You wasted lots of great rides worrying about nothing."

"That I did."
"Are you enjoying your ride today, dear?"
"More than you will ever know Peter."
Smiling to himself, Peter thought, just maybe, there was hope for them after all.

Peter and Sharon rode for over two hours before they ended up back at home. Peter knew Sharon would be some sore tomorrow, if not by tonight.

They came around the barn on one side, and Jessy and Mitch came around from the other side.

"Hi Dad, Mom. Did you have a good ride?"
"I think we did. Did we, Sharon?"
"Yes, we had a great ride." As Sharon went to swing her leg over the saddle to get off, her muscles started to scream in pain. The pain she began to feel was her worst nightmare.

"Oh my," she said as she sort of hung on the saddle. Peter was already off his horse and was making his way around to help Sharon when he had heard the pain in her voice.

"Let me help you, dear." He reached up and took her around her waist and lifted her down. Sharon just sort of slid down Peter's body to the ground. Although she was in pain, she could also feel the arousal it had caused in Peter. Never mind what it had done to her. To still have such an impact like this on Peter and on herself after all these years made her feel a little weak in the knees.

"Are you okay, sweetheart?"
"Yes, Peter. My knees are a little weak from the ride. They will recover, thank you." She then turned away, not wanting Peter to see the effect he still held over her.

"Are we going to have lunch before you leave, Sharon?"

"Yes, I will go up and make something while you put the horses away. Perhaps that is all my knees will need to get back under me."

"Thank you. I won't be long." Peter would do anything he could to get Sharon to stay longer. If only he felt secure enough to ask her to move back home. There had to be a way without spoiling what they have. He knew he could live forever on what they have, so was it selfish to want more? He felt in his heart that it could be so much better. At one point, he thought of asking Jessy her thoughts on it, but not wanting to get her hopes up or wanting to open old wounds for her, he choose not to. This was something he would have to do alone and figure out what would be best for all of them.

His heart would ache once again the moment Sharon pulled out of the driveway. He had gotten to hate her good-byes. Peter found himself moping around after Sharon would leave, and that was not him. At one time, he would just keep busy and he felt happy to know that in a few days she would be back, but none of this was doing it for him. He found that he just became a lonely man each time she would leave.

Tending to the horses was something he did now because he had to, not because he enjoyed it anymore. The moments with Sharon was all he lived for. Counting the days till she would be back was the highlight of his days. Peter sat many hours on his veranda daydreaming of what had once been and what he wished would be again. He would enjoy his private times even if it were just in his dreams. For now, he would go up to the house and bathe in her scent and hold on to every moment they could share.

At first Peter scolded himself for letting himself be so weak when it came to Sharon, but as time went on, he couldn't help but miss her and feel they were wasting precious time. After all, they weren't getting any younger.

When he went to pull the barn door open, he could hear Jessy and Mitch talking and laughing outside. God, what he would do to have that again. It made him smile, yet it also made his heart ache as he and Sharon once had what they have now. Was this something you only had while you were young? Could he and Sharon get it back, or was it too late?

Opening the door and seeing Jessy with hay in her hair and a smile as wide as the sky warmed Peter's heart. His daughter had found love even if she didn't want to admit it. He only hoped that the two of them would get their crap together before they became too old to know what they had missed. Surely neither of them would drag this on for years as he and Sharon had done.

Then it hit him like a ton of bricks: Jessy wouldn't know any different, would she? The way her mother and he had lived may be the only way she thought it would work.

"God, I must talk to her," he said to himself. At least he thought he had.

"You say something, Dad?"

"No, just talking to myself. At my age, it happens."

"Okay. Are you headed to the house now?"

"Yes, I am. I'm starving."

"Well, Mom will have lunch ready by now."

"Hope she has made lots. Riding makes a man hungry."

Wrapping her arm around her dad's waist and snuggling in to get the scent of his cologne always made her feel safe. She said to him, "Mom always makes plenty. Let me help you so you don't collapse from starvation." The three of them laughed all the way to the house.

Jessy was right. Sharon had made soup and sandwiches, and there was plenty. Jessy knew it was for her dad's benefit so he would have some for supper when they all left at the end of the day. Jessy had gotten the feeling the last couple times she was leaving that her dad didn't want them leaving. He didn't seem to handle it as easy as he once had.

She had mentioned it to Mitch. Mitch, of course, thought she was just being overly motherly when it came to her dad. He would tell her, *"You know, Jessy, you can't be his wife or his mother. You are his daughter."*

That didn't stop Jessy from worrying about her dad and being sad for him. She too understood that he was getting older and perhaps a little lonely, especially in the evenings when his day's work was done and he went into an empty house.

Jessy had realized it after Mitch had spent some time with her at the farm then going home to her apartment. When she would close her apartment door, it was an empty, lonely feeling that would wash over her. How had she lived like that for so long? Four walls to talk to, to share the day with. For herself, she knew in the morning she would be in the company of the man she enjoyed. The truth be told, it was the man she loved. Unlike her father, as he would have to face another day alone.

She knew her parents still had feelings for each other, but nothing strong enough to bring them back together as one. That thought made her sad as she hugged her father good-bye and saw the sadness in his eyes.

Chapter 15

The last six months had gone by so fast. Jessy didn't know how it had done so. She could only chalk it up to Mitch, and knowing she was spending another day with him always made her look forward to tomorrow.

They had had to deal with some horrible accidents though. There was the one where a load of logs broke loose from the truck, wiping out the biker who was riding beside him. The man was so badly mangled it was hard to find him among the logs. A cherry picker had been used to pick the logs up. It took some time for them to be able to find the bike and the man that had been riding it.

There were two teenage girls in a car behind him who had gone into shock with what they had witnessed.

Blake Eastmen was his name, and he was fifty-eight years old. His sister had said he was taking a trip across Canada wanting to find out where he would settle at the time of his retirement. He was a single man with no children. This was a sad thought, yet in a way, it was also a blessing. His parents were both gone, and he had the one sister who was older than he was. They were very close.

The grief she would carry would be hard on a person her age. Perhaps it would never heal.

The cross that Jessy would put up for Blake would carry a bike helmet. Some things helmets just don't protect you from. It was all in God's hands today for Blake.

Mitch had a bike stored away, and in the week to follow this tragic death, Mitch sold his bike. He knew from what Jessy had said after the accident that he would never get her on the bike. He no longer wanted to ride alone. Selling his bike made him feel guilty after what he had just dealt with, but he also knew that freak accidents happen. He could only pray that the young man who bought his bike would have nothing but enjoyment with his newfound love.

Love was something he never thought he would find again. He knew his first love wasn't love. At that age, it was all about sex. What he felt for Jessy, well, he was sure it was love. Yet he was scared to act on his feelings, driving her away, and spoiling what they had wasn't something he was willing to take a chance with. It had taken him a long time to get to this point, and thinking about it, he didn't know how it could be any better.

He and Jessy spent quality time together as well as worked together. They seem to know what the other was thinking and what the other would answer before they answered. Many times they had answered the same way at the same time. How could two people think the same and still get along? It took Mitch a long time to admit to himself that he loved Jessy. She had slipped into his heart without hesitation, and he knew this girl was meant for him. All of her. Their restraint had allowed his love to grow beyond his expectations.

ROAD SIDE CROSSES

Mitch knew he was in it for the long haul. He wasn't sure about Jessy. Her life was work, and she made it quite clear many times. Although they wanted many of the same things out of life, he knew he didn't dare push. After all, what was the rush? They were young, and neither of them was going anywhere. That made him think of Peter and Sharon.

Talking about not going anywhere, he couldn't understand their relationship but wouldn't ask Jessy. He wasn't going to open any wounds. Jessy had mentioned her concerns about her parents from time to time, and Mitch would just say. "I'm sure they will figure it out." He didn't have any answers for her. He wanted to be her sounding board and a shoulder if she needed one, but as far as advice, he would just as soon step aside and let someone else offer her that. All he felt he could do for the woman he loved so deeply was to pray for her and her dream of her parents moving back in under the same roof. He really hoped this was something that would happen before life passed them by and they would regret the choice they had made. He knew they were both proud people and a little strong minded. There was no doubt this was in their way. It was holding them back, or was it?

He made a mental note of trying to talk to Peter about how they live. He would have to figure out how to ask without meddling. Maybe he would be able to swing a conversation over to take that in. Couldn't hurt to try. Not that it was any of his business, really, but he got to thinking about Jessy. Perhaps she would always want to live the way they were because of her parents.

"*God, that would suck,*" he mumbled to himself as Jessy came around the corner.

"Are you talking to yourself?"

"Yeah. I thought you got lost, so I was getting lonely and had to start talking to myself."

Laughing, she punched him lightly in the arm, saying, "Come, partner. I have our coffees. Now let's get back to the station and do our paperwork."

"Yes, let's."

They had had smaller mishaps since the bike wreck. The ones that stuck in his mind was the one of a young woman in labor for the first time, and watching Jessy with her was amazing. One would have thought Jessy had had children of her own. She was a pro at talking anyway.

The second one was an elderly man with chest pains. He was out cleaning his sidewalk. He also lived alone. It was a good thing someone was passing by at the same time as he collapsed to the ground.

This was what got Mitch thinking about being alone for the rest of his life, but until now, it had been fine with him. Now he wanted more. He wanted to share the rest of his life with Jessy. She made him laugh, and she made him feel alive. He had not known how dead he was. It had just become his way of life, and people slide into their way of living without thought of tomorrow. The transformation was a slow, smooth one, and you didn't realize the fun in life you are shutting out. Good Lord, he was actually a walking dead man until he met Jessy. What had she seen in such a boring person?

When he thought about it, Jessy was living the same as he had been. All work and very little play. Yes, she had her veterinarian practice on the side, but it was still just work. It didn't matter how much she enjoyed it or how you looked at it—it was still work.

"Mitch, is something wrong?"

Jerking his head up with a frown, he said, "No, why do you ask?"

"You have been off in la-la land most of the day."

"I'm sorry."

"Have I done something you're not happy with? I had to use the bathroom, that's why I took so long at Timmy's."

He was laughing now and shaking his head. "No, Jessy, you have not done anything. I'm glad you used the bathroom. Wouldn't want a mess to clean up."

They both laughed.

"So what's up?"

"Nothing, really. Just deep in thought today is all."

"Oh my, must be serious."

"Yeah and no"

"You want to talk about it?"

"No, nothing to talk about. Just thoughts. Thanks for asking. Are we still going bowling tonight?"

"Yeah, if you want to?"

"I was thinking, why don't you ask your mom and dad to join us? Do they bowl?"

"They used to take me bowling, and they were good at it. So yeah, I will call them and see what they are up to."

"Sounds great. I'm going to check out and go home to shower. How about you?"

"I just have to hand in my report, and I'm out of here."

"All right. See you at seven." He turned to leave.

"Mitch."

"Yeah, Jess?"

"Are you sure you're okay?"

"Yes, Jess, I'm fine." He went back over and kissed her on the top of the head. She had wished he would have kissed her on her lips, but it was something they have never done at work.

Her guts were telling her something wasn't right with Mitch. It wasn't like him not to talk to her about what he had on his mind. They had gotten to where they shared every thought, good or bad, and every dream. So why wouldn't he share now?

She replayed the whole day over in her head and didn't see anything that would shut him down, so she started to go over their last week together. There wasn't anything she missed, yet there was nothing jumping out at her telling her what had Mitch sitting back and being so quiet. Quiet was not him. He loved to talk and had always been interesting to listen too. He would even get her arguing with him just for the fun of it. Then it hit her.

Oh my god. Mitch is being transferred.

Chapter 16

Jessy felt she had the weight of the world now on her shoulders. When had he gotten the notice, and why wouldn't he talk to her about it?

Jessy went home and got ready to go bowling. All the time, everything seemed to be moving in slow motion. What would she do? How could she go on without Mitch in her life every day? Who would she have for a partner now? God, she didn't want anyone else. Where was Mitch going? Would he be too far away for them to continue their friendship?

"Damn it, anywhere but here is too far away," Jessy said as she put her keys into her pocket. Mitch should be there any moment to pick her up.

Should she wait for him to tell her, or should she just jump in with both feet and beg him to stay? This wasn't her, and she had no idea when Mitch had gotten embedded so deeply into her heart. How had she allowed it to happen?

This was one of the reasons she stayed clear of deep relationships. They hurt like hell when things went south.

Perhaps she could put in for a transfer as well. Yes, she would check it out. Slapping herself on the side of the head, she said, "Wake up, Jessy, you can't chase a man around." If he felt anything for her, he would have not agreed to go. Now this had her thinking in a different direction. Mitch didn't care for her as much as she had thought. Had she made a fool of herself all this time thinking she had won him over and that his feelings for her were genuine?

How many times had her dad told her to be careful, and to go slow? Her answer was always the same: *"Dad, if we go any slower, hell will freeze over."*

"It had been three years since Mitch had been transferred there. They both lost sight that he more than her could get a transfer at any time after six months. She was what was considered a home-based hire and only transferred out on a request.

Did Mitch request a transfer after all this time? Could it be he didn't know how to handle his feelings for her? Either way, it wasn't sitting well with Jessy.

The doorbell rang.

The ride to the bowling lanes was quiet on Jessy's side of the truck. Mitch had found his tongue and was talking up a storm, but Jessy heard very little of what he was saying. In fact, she was on the verge of crying. This was something else she didn't like about relationships. It made strong people weak.

"Hey, Jess, something wrong?"

Shaking her head until she could find a strong voice that wouldn't be all cracked up with tears, she spoke, "No, guess I'm just tired now."

"You should have said something. We could have stayed home and watched a movie."

"It will be great to spend time with Mom and Dad."

"Oh, for sure. I do enjoy their company. They are a very interesting couple."

It was funny because Jessy never thought of them in any other way but as a couple. It made her think about how other people saw them. Did their neighbors still think of them as a couple, or was it just her? Were they talked about like other divorced couples? She had never heard anything come back to her about what someone had said about her parents.

"Speaking of the couple."

"Hi, Mom. Hi, Dad."

"Hi. Have you two been waiting long?"

"No, Dad, we just got here, like, five minutes ago."

"All right. Your mother and I will get our shoes."

After they were all suited up with their shirts and shoes, they had a marvelous time. At break time, Jessy and Sharon went to get them all drinks, so Mitch thought he would ask the question that had been haunting him.

"Peter, may I ask you something?"

"You sure can, son. Glad to help if I can."

"Do you think you and Sharon will ever get your act together and be under the same roof again as husband and wife?"

This took Peter by surprise. It wasn't at all what he thought Mitch would be asking. Not that he knew what it was, but this? With a frown, he looked at Mitch for a bit before he answered.

"I'm sorry if I'm out of line. It just seems like such a waste. You two are together every time you can be, so why not live together again? You seem to get along great. There is definitely love between you. The sparks fly every time you two are in a room together."

"Well, Mitch, it's not that I haven't thought about it, 'cause I have been, but God, man, I have to say I'm scared of spoiling what we have. There is nothing I want more than for my wife to be in my bed every night and to wake up to her every morning. I'm scared to take the chance, and ask her to move back. If it isn't what she wants, then she may just pull away, and if I ask and she says no, I know my heart will break. Life will not be as good as it is now."

"Good as it is now, you are a sad man, Peter. It is written all over your face. Your daughter sees it all the time, and it hurts her to see the pain in your eyes."

"Pain or no pain, I don't want to lose what I have right now with Sharon. She is my life. She is the reason I get up every morning."

"Have you told her that?"

"Not in so many words."

"So why don't you? Feel her out, I mean."

"Mitch, I get there is more to this than just Sharon and I. What's up?"

Now it was Mitch that sat in silence.

"Well, spill the beans, son. I told you, now come clean."

"I'm wondering if the way you and Sharon are living will be the only way Jessy will want to live. Not that there is anything wrong with the way you are living. I just don't think it's for everyone."

"What do you have in mind?"

Just at that moment, the girls came back. Jessy picked up on it right away. "Hey, why so serious? Thought we were here for a good time?"

"That we are, love." Mitch took his drink from Jessy's hand.

Peter couldn't help but see the love in Mitch's eyes. That man loved his daughter as much as he loved his wife. Now it all made sense. Was he wanting to marry his daughter, or was he thinking that Jessy would be fine with living the way her parents were? Perhaps he just wanted to live in common law with his daughter. Either way, wasn't what Peter had dreamed of for his daughter? Yet who was he to criticize?

The bowling was great, and at the end, they all went to Timmy's for coffee and donuts.

"This is something we should do more often," Sharon said as she looked at the faces of her opponents whose butts she had just kicked.

"That would be great, Mom. What do you say, Dad? Are you up for this?"

"Of course. I can't think of anything else I would rather do."

"Settled then."

"Looks that way," Mitch said as he tilted his head, giving Jessy an evil eye. He would find out later what she was up to.

"Well, we had better get home. Morning comes early, and we are back on duty. We are to get more snow, so it will be busy with all sorts of mishaps."

"Okay, dear, I will call you tomorrow." Sharon turned to hug and kiss Jessy good night then sat back down.

Peter was pleased to see she wasn't rushing off home. He didn't want to go home—not alone anyway.

"Snow does bring out the silly drivers, all right." Seeing how they were talking about snow, Peter thought it would be a good time to bring up Christmas. After all, it wasn't far away. Sharon loved Christmas. She made it so special for everyone. It was like a fairy tale come true.

"Sharon, are you doing Christmas this year?"

That brought a frown as she looked at Peter. "Of course. Don't I do it every year? Unless you or Jessy are doing it all this year."

Peter knew it was a dumb question, but he just wanted to make conversation. He wasn't ready to let her go yet. "No, I'm not, and I don't think Jessy is, but I sure would love to help you."

"I know you do, Peter. I love you for that."

"What colors you doing this year?"

"I think we will do the old Christmas, red and green. With a touch of gold."

"That's one of my favorites. It is old Christmas, for sure." Peter wanted to say, "Do blue and white." That was how he was feeling. Call it a blue Christmas. He knew he would spend it with her and Jessy, but damn it, it was not the same.

Peter was thinking ahead to when it snowed. He was coming in, and he was going to take Sharon out walking in the snow. There was nothing more romantic than large flakes coming down on a warm winter's evening. He and Sharon had loved walking in many snowstorms. Sometimes, they were the only ones out on those evenings, when they would go into town just to walk the streets.

The snow coming down heavy over the streetlights would soften the glow of the lights and take them back in time. It always made them feel like they were back in the thirties. They never knew why, it just did. It would remind them of the old days. So many Christmas cards would have that scene on them, and it was always breathtaking.

Sharon had mentioned a time or two how she and Peter must be old souls. The old days were always something they felt their spirits were tied to, as if they had been reincarnated. So many times Sharon had told Peter she wished she had lived back then when life was simple yet hard.

The memory Peter had of Sharon trying to catch snowflakes with her mouth brought a chuckle deep inside. She had done that every year they were together and always loved it. Of course they stopped along the way and made snow angels. They always had a blast.

He also remembered the fourth winter with Jessy and how the three of them had spent all one weekend building a snow fort. They had always loved wintertime. Winter was great for the people who got outside and enjoyed it. Could he get her to do that again? Could they get back and enjoy what they once had?

Chapter 17

Their coffee time came to an end, and so did Peter's daydreaming. It was time to take Sharon home. He would do this with great regret yet never show her he was anything but happy. Taking her in his arms and holding her was so easy, and it seemed to be the right thing to do. They were meant to be together. Otherwise, why hadn't they taken other partners? He could make all kinds of excuses, but nothing was the truth other than in his heart Sharon was still his wife.

There had not been another woman who touched his heart as Sharon had, and he totally believed in the fact that there is only one true love for you in this world and in your lifetime. Sharon was his. He thought back on the women who would flirt with him at the cattle shows and how easy it would have been to take them to his bed. But in the morning, he would have had nothing but regrets, and right now, the only regret he wanted to live with was not having Sharon in his bed every night and waking up beside him. It was easier for him to walk away from temptation than to sacrifice any chance of rebuilding what he and Sharon had had.

At first, he believed that he and Sharon stayed the way they were for their daughter's sake. Trying to give her a steady, balanced life. Seeing her grow up and making her dreams come true without the hassle of their divorce. It wasn't long before he knew within his heart he would love no other, and so if Sharon never came home, he would die a lonely man.

Kissing Sharon good night and releasing her brought pain.

"Good night, Peter," Sharon said as she placed her hand upon his cheek. His eyes had gotten darker with sadness. This tore at her heart. When would this man let go of his pride? When would he make things right? He had the power to take the sadness away, or at least she had hoped she knew what put such sadness in his eyes.

"Good night, sweetheart. I will call you tomorrow."

"All right, dear. Talk to you then. Sleep well."

She didn't think that was happening anytime soon. As Peter turned to walk away, Sharon wanted to grab at his arm and ask him to stay. It wasn't her pride that stopped her but fear. Did she want more than he was willing to give? Was the sadness she saw in his eyes caused by her, or was it something else? Could Peter have a health issue? She knew his business was well, for she did his books. So if it wasn't his health, then it had to be her. He hadn't said a word about not being well, and the evenings they had spent together were nothing more than unbelievable.

Was that what was standing in her way? Was she afraid that their sex life would suffer if she asked to move back home? Would they become too complacent with each other or perhaps take each other for granted? That was not what she would want their lives to become. She loved what they had. She was just so damn lonely the nights they were apart, and waking up in the morning alone wasn't the way she wanted to start her day.

Dragging your body around all day, waiting for the phone to ring, and hoping it was Peter on the other end was getting to be annoying.

Perhaps she could talk to Jessy and get her take on this. Jessy sometimes had good feelings about her father that Sharon had overlooked. She may have noticed the sadness in her father's eyes and may have some ideas of why. They hadn't had many mother-and-daughter days since Mitch came into Jessy's life.

Sitting down on the edge of her bed made her think. Now that was so sad. Why had she let it go so long? She knew Jessy and Mitch spent most of their time together, but why had she stepped aside so easily and let him take her time away from her daughter?

Sharon shook her head in disappointment with herself. She knew the answer to her own question. She was pining for Peter, and when you were pining for someone, no one else mattered. Spending time with Jessy would be the first thing she planned for on Jessy's next days off. So she would call her tomorrow and set up a date and time.

Sharon had dropped many of her clients. She had a few that would take a little longer to clear up then she was shutting it down. She would be fifty-eight this year, and she wanted to go home and enjoy the rest of her days being Peter's wife. She had remembered Jessy telling them about Mr. Eastmen who was dead at fifty-eight. So to think people had all the time in the world was just plan crazy.

It was more like here today and gone tomorrow. So she would give Peter until the New Year. If he hadn't asked her to move home by then, she would take the bull by the horns and ask if she could go home.

So she had started planning ahead of time and dropping her clients and be ready to close the doors by the end of January 2000. After all, 2000 was to be the year of great new happenings although some people thought it would mean devastation for the world.

Sharon never held much to anyone's claims. She would wake up every day and just take it one day at a time. She would make sure she was with Peter and Jessy on New Year's Eve in case something was to go wrong. In that case, the three of them would still be together. She had happier thoughts of 2000, and she was going to do whatever it took to see them come true.

It was known that if you had a dream and you sat idle, it was not going to happen. Dreams don't just drop in your lap. You have to have a dream then you have to work hard to see that dream come true. Sharon was never a big dreamer. She never dreamed of far out-of-the-way places. Sharon always said she wasn't interested in looking for trouble and was quite happy to stay put and never longed for anything in her life, except Peter.

That longing will be coming to an end very soon. That thought put a smile on her face. She was going to bed happy, after all.

Sharon woke to the doorbell ringing. Rolling over and seeing it was only 6 a.m. made her stomach do flips and her blood run cold. Who the hell would be at her door this early? Grabbing her house coat and pushing her hair out of her eyes, she ran to the door. She opened it quickly then stood there with her mouth open. It took a bit before she could say anything.

"Peter, what's wrong? Is Jessy okay?"

"Yes, sweetheart. As far as I know, she is."

"Then why are you here so early? Something wrong?"

"Nothing wrong, my love. I couldn't sleep, so I'm taking you for breakfast."

"Look! I'm not ready to go for breakfast."

"I can see that, and I didn't expect you to be. I will wait, unless you don't want to go. Then I'm sorry I have bothered you."

"Oh, it's no bother, Peter. I would love to go for breakfast with you. Just give me some time. You know if you would have called, I would have been ready."

"I thought about calling, but I didn't want to give you room to turn me down. You're always so busy."

Sharon thought, *If he only knew.* "Yes, I guess I am. So this is good." Sharon reached out and took his hand.

"I will be just a bit."

"Take your time. I'm in no rush, unless you are?"

"Me, in a rush this early? Never." Sharon laughed as she headed for the bedroom to get dressed.

Peter went and sat on the sofa. He hadn't stayed very often over at Sharon's. He never wanted her to feel pressured, so he would wait until she came to the farm. He knew then it would be something she wanted.

Sharon came out of the bedroom half an hour later and was nervous as hell. Sharon didn't know why. She just was. "I'm ready Peter."

Peter stood up and turned to face Sharon. She never failed to take his breath away. "Wow, you look amazing."

"Now, Peter, it's nothing."

"Nothing? You should be going somewhere really fancy for breakfast, not the corner cafe."

"Peter, it's a sweater and slacks. Nothing special."

"Aw, sweetheart, you deserve so much more." Peter leaned over and kissed her cheek.

"No, Peter, I don't. I'm just me, and we are going for breakfast. I think you need to go out more."

"Hey, I'm up to that if you are."

"Peter, you're impossible." Sharon snuggled into his side.

"Yeah, so you have told me." Peter chuckled as he kissed the top of her head. Taking her out to the truck, he asked, "Is there someplace else you would rather go, Sharon?"

"No, the corner cafe is fine, Peter."

"The corner cafe it is then."

Their breakfast was great as always, and conversation was great. What more could a man ask for?

Some things had never changed. Many of the old faces were still coming to the corner café, where their first dreams of the future had been discussed and now perhaps dreams of retirement would be the topic.

"Sharon, what are your plans for retirement? Do you have any, or is it too soon for you to think of retiring?"

"I have been thinking about it lots. Just not sure what will happen yet. I don't think it's too early to plan. Making your plans come true is a different story."

"I hear you. Could be tough, hey?"

Chapter 18

The wet snow was falling, and it was somewhat foggy out. The air had been damp, so the fog hung in the air like a curtain. You would not want to be traveling fast or far in these conditions. It made visibility very poor.

Peter and Sharon were deep in conversation when they saw the cops go flying by. Behind them was unit 1204. It was Mitch and Jessy's unit.

"Looks like the kids have a big job ahead of them."

"I would say the chances of it being a good one is slim. Not when it is in need of all them," Sharon said as she pointed to the fire rescue trucks just coming around the corner.

"I would think you're right. Gosh, I don't know how our daughter handles this job so well."

"It does take special people. Guess our daughter is one of them."

"She is very special to me, anyways."

"To us, Sharon."

"Yes, to us. Peter, have you ever been sorry you didn't have more children?"

"Not sorry, Sharon, but it would have been nice to have had a son, perhaps. Jessy has done a great job as far as filling my parenting skills."

"Jessy was an easy child to raise."

"Yes, she was, my point exactly. Perhaps another would have given us grief neither one of us would have wanted."

"Especially with us being divorced."

"Not all children would have handled it as well as Jessy did."

"Us having another child might have made all the difference to the outcome."

"Yes, having just Jessy to deal with made it so much less complicated. Although that is a selfish reason not to have more children, or at least one more."

"Well, my dear, it is too late to think of that."

"Nothing like the fun trying, and you're never too old for that."

"That is true, Peter. Do you think we have had a fulfilled life to this point?"

Peter thought on this a minute. Knowing how he felt deep down and knowing what Sharon would probably want to hear, he opted for the latter.

"To this point in our lives, I think so."

"Any regrets, Peter?"

God, this was getting to tough and dangerous. Was he going to put it all on the table or play his hand tight to his chest as all poker players do?

"Regrets, Sharon? I guess we all have regrets of some kind. How about you?"

Sharon now wondered how she would answer her own question. "Yeah, Peter, I guess you're right. Everyone will have regrets of some kind to deal with. Some are harder than others."

"You know the only way to live with regret is to change what has caused the regret, if you can."

Now Sharon was looking so deeply into those beautiful blue eyes. The ones that were sad and were full of regret. She wondered if Peter could see the same as he sat there and looked as deeply into her eyes. She felt like he could read regret written on her forehead as well as see it overflowing from her eyes every time she had shed a tear. Which was very close to happening at this very moment.

Sharon bowed her head and dug in her purse for a Kleenex, helping her to regain her composure.

"Are you all right, Sharon?"

"Yes, Peter, I'm just fine. Thank you."

Peter could see that their conversation was getting to her, so he thought changing the subject would be best. "No one has come back from the wreck. It must be out of town a fair ways."

"We will have to call Jessy to see how things went." Jessy called in every day just so that her parents knew she was fine. Sharon new she wouldn't have to call Jessy. She just didn't know what else to say.

Not without pouring her heart out to Peter and this she couldn't gamble on right now to make a fool of herself. To become one of those women who would cry and beg for the man to take her back wasn't in Sharon's genes. Nor would her pride allow her to act in such a manner.

With Christmas not far away, she wouldn't want anything to spoil it for Jessy or for Peter and herself. Nor would she want to be on the outs with Peter at Christmastime. They had not had any issues for so long it was like they were one. Oh, God, to be one again, to be a couple. Sharon would give almost anything to see that happen. She wasn't willing to lose what they had to bring it up to Peter. So she would go through Christmas with a heavy heart although she knew they would be together. Just not in the way she wanted them to be.

"Well, my dear, the fog is finally lifting, so I must go home and feed the cattle, now that I can see where I will be going."

"Yes, I better get to the books today, or I will be too far behind to enjoy it."

"Do you still enjoy it as much as you used too?"

"It's not the same, no. How about you and farming?"

"No, it seems like it's more work than I remember." Peter laughed as they got up from the table.

"Guess when you're young, everything is easier, hey?"

"You saying I'm old?"

"No, dear, you're not a young stud anymore either."

"I can still perform as a young stud. I will show you later."

"You will?"

"Yeah, I will come in and we will go to the movies. How about that? We haven't done that in a while."

"That sounds nice, Peter."

"Okay, it's a date, but now I must drop you off and head home and get my daily chores done. Jumper will be wondering where I got to."

"He's doing great."

"Yes, the old boy came through very well, thanks to Jessy. I won't use him as hard as I used to. He deserves to be cared for now. He has given me many years of pleasure, and he has worked hard for me. It's time for his retirement as well."

"You really thinking of retiring, Peter?"

"It won't be far away, Sharon. I would like to just enjoy some other things besides the farm before I am too old to do so."

"The cattle and the horse have always been your life, Peter. You love what you do."

"There are other things I love more, like spending time with you."

"I love that too, Peter. Thank you for breakfast. Next one is on me, okay?"

"That's a deal."

Peter hoped for what he had in mind: she would be cooking him breakfast tomorrow morning.

As they drove away, they saw the tow truck coming in with a vehicle on the back that no one could identify. The fire rescue was right behind him.

"Oh my gosh, that doesn't look good at all."

"To think of it, we haven't even heard sirens come back to town."

"That isn't good news."

"I'm sure Jessy will fill us in."

"Me too. Perhaps we can go see her before the movie."

"Yeah, we could do that, if I get home and get done what all I have to do. Your bad for me, Sharon, you make me forget the time. You always have."

"Don't blame me because you're weak, Peter," Sharon said as she shut the truck door. She waved at him as he drove away.

Trust Sharon to get the last word in. She had always done that. It was like she would give Peter something to think about while they were apart. There were times when he needed to do just that, and this was one of them. All the way home, he thought of what it was that he could get his wife for Christmas.

Perhaps they should take a long trip. He knew Sharon was not a traveler, so this could prove to be a problem. Sharon was happy being at home, surrounded by what she loved. That thought put a frown on his face. The only thing she was surrounded with right now was paperwork. That can't be all she would want to be happy with.

Peter made a note in his mind that he would ask Jessy. Jessy would know what he should buy for his wife. She had helped him out many times in the past. Not that Peter didn't know what his wife liked, but making the decision when he would have too many choices to choose from was hard. Jessy would always pick for him. Peter was good with that. He would make the choices, and then get Jessy to do the final pick. At least the choices were of his picking, not the salesclerk's or his daughter's. Sometimes he would buy both 'cause Jessy couldn't decide either. She always told her dad if he didn't have such good taste it wouldn't be so hard.

Peter loved Christmas. He loved how Sharon's eyes would light up and the sparkle that would be in them all over Christmas. This Christmas, for some reason, he was having trouble thinking of what his wife would like. What could he buy her that would make her eyes sparkle from here to eternity? What would make her heart skip a beat if only for a brief moment? He really hoped Jessy had some ideas. This had to be the first year Peter was pulling a blank.

Peter worked hard and steady all day, yet he couldn't get Sharon off his mind for five minutes. He felt foolish. It wasn't like he was a teenager. She had consumed his every thought then as well. Even having lots to do, he found the day dragging on. *Maybe I should take my watch off. Looking at it every half hour isn't helping.*

Peter was getting frustrated with himself. He knew he would be headed into town long before he needed to. He would just have to find something to do while waiting to pick up Sharon. He would give his truck a good scrubbing. That would kill some time.

Sharon had her book work done by noon. She was spending time in the tub and making sure everything about herself would be pleasing to Peter's eyes and smell. She had even put a light color in her hair. It was so close to her own color, but it gave her hair the healthy shine she wanted. She had often thought of getting her hair cut. Knowing Peter loved her hair long, that was how she would wear it although menopause was making it tough to keep long. She wore it up most of the time as she couldn't take the heat on her neck. Whoever said it was all great after fifty had no idea what they were talking about. Menopause causes many things to change in a woman's body. Some are very challenging, to say the least.

Sharon painted her toenails a very vibrant red to match her fingernails. She was wearing red to go out for supper and the show, and she had bought a new silk nightgown with a housecoat that she would wear that evening. It matched her nail color perfectly.

Peter loved to see her in red. He had always told her that red was her color. She was hoping to persuade Peter to stay the night. It had been quite a while since Peter had stayed over with her. She had often wondered why yet never got around to asking him. Peter wasn't a man who enjoyed anyplace but the farm. So she had come to the conclusion that was all it was about. She would never get Peter to leave the farm.

Not that she wanted to. Sharon loved being at the farm as well. It was hard to leave and go back to her little house in town. She did feel the little house was all they needed. With no grandchildren, why a big house? The ranch-style house was their dream home, and Peter wouldn't start with anything smaller. At one time, they had talked about having four kids and the space they would need. With only half of that dream coming true.

Chapter 19

"Wow, very pretty."

"Thank you. Come in, I will get my coat." Sharon brought her coat out, and Peter took it from her hands.

"May I do the honors?"

"You sure can. Thank you."

"Should we go and eat before we see Jessy?"

"Maybe we should pop in before in case we run late eating. Wouldn't want to miss the beginning of the movie."

"Have you heard from Jessy?"

"No, you either?"

"No."

"That's not like her."

"They probably had a long day with that accident."

"Nothing much was on the news, which I don't get. Seeing how it called for the fire rescue trucks as well."

"She will tell us."

"Okay. Let's stop for a moment to see her. She won't mind."

"Her eyes always light right up whenever she sees the two of us together. Sometimes I think we are being cruel to her."

"Why is that, Peter?"

"You know our little girl would like nothing more than to see us back together."

"Peter, if you think about it, we really haven't been apart."

"In her eyes, we are." He wanted to say in his eyes as well but thought he best stop it right there. Upsetting Sharon wasn't in his plans tonight, or any other night, for that matter.

Mitch's truck was at Jessy's. This wasn't anything new, and it never surprised either Peter or Sharon.

"Well, looks like we get to visit them both. Two for the price of one."

"Hope we aren't interrupting anything."

When they knocked, Mitch answered the door.

"Hey, Mitch." Man, he looked awful, and right away, Sharon was sick to her stomach. Had they caught them having a fight?

"Come in."

Peter and Sharon looked at each other then back at Mitch.

"Hey, man, if this is a bad time, we can come back another day."

"You're probably just what Jessy needs. Come in, please. Jessy is on the sofa. I was just making some soup."

"Is Jessy sick?" Sharon asked as she entered the living room. Jessy was crying, and there was a bucket beside the sofa.

"Oh, sweetheart, what is wrong?" Sharon said as she sat down beside her, and Peter made his way to her side. Jessy just buried her face into Sharon's chest and cried so hard. Tears were flowing from both Sharon and Peter.

As Mitch came in with the soup, Peter got up off the sofa and was on him like a raped ape.

"Good God, man, what has happened that Jessy would be so upset? Are you two fighting?"

"Fighting?" Mitch went white in the face. "No, sir, we're not fighting."

"Then please tell us what the hell has our daughter so upset."

Mitch put the soup down on the coffee table as he said to Jessy, "Come on, babe, please try to eat something. You have to, Jess, or you will get sick."

Jessy just shook her head. "If I do, I will be sick again."

"Oh, honey, have you been to a doctor?"

"She doesn't need a doctor. She needs time. Lots of time."

"What? Why?" Peter was frowning and looking at Mitch.

Then Mitch started in slowly. "The accident we dealt with today was very bad. In fact, that doesn't even come close to describing it. It was something from a horror show."

"We saw all the fire rescue trucks going out. We knew it had to be bad," Peter said as he took his seat beside his daughter.

"What can we do to help, sweetheart?"

"There is nothing you can do, Dad." She laid her head into his side.

Mitch continued to tell them what had happened. "It was an older van with four kids and their parents. The kids were all under ten years of age. With the fog, they didn't see the pipe truck that had jackknifed in the road. The van hit the truck, ripping it open like a tin can. The pipe went through the van killing them all."

"Oh my god," Sharon said as she put her hand over her mouth. She felt her stomach do a flip.

Peter just hung his head, not knowing what he could do to make his daughter or Mitch feel any better. "Aw, man, I'm sorry."

"Not your fault, Peter. The weather was to blame. Although they weren't traveling fast, but hitting something that big at any speed was going to be a killer."

"The whole family wiped out. Thank God for that, I guess."

Sharon pulled Jessy closer to her side. "Mitch is right, sweetheart. You have to eat."

"Mom, I can't. All I see is blood everywhere and bodies that had been torn apart."

Sharon's stomach did another flip as she recalled the accident she had witnessed with Jessy and how it had bothered her for months after they got home. How every time she closed her eyes all she could see was blood. That was only with two people involved. What it must be like to see it with six?

"Even their dog was killed, Mom."

"Aw, Jessy, I'm so sorry you had to witness such a horrifying scene."

"Mom."

"What is it, Jessy? There's something you're not telling. What has you so upset? You have dealt with death of both young and old and have had some very messed-up accidents. Why has this one gotten to you so badly?"

"He was beheaded, Mom. The father of those children."

Sharon's color drained from her face instantly, and as she looked over at Peter, she saw he had lost all his color as well. Sharon felt the room start to spin, and Peter was at her side before she hit the floor. He lay her down on the sofa beside Jessy and talked to her to keep her awake while Mitch brought a cold cloth to put on Sharon's forehead. He was watching Peter tend to his wife. He could tell Peter was having a hard time swallowing what he had just been told.

"Peter, let me tend to Sharon. You better just sit and take some deep breaths."

"God, Mitch, that had to be just awful for you and Jessy. Why didn't you call us? We would have come right away."

"We know you would have. Jessy and I needed time to digest it ourselves."

"Was this your first time witnessing such a thing, Mitch?"

"Yes, sir."

"Oh, son, I'm sorry, but I have to say I'm glad you were there for our daughter."

"I am too. Jessy did very well considering we just talked to each other and kept focus on everything that was going on around us. I could tell Jessy was in trouble, and keeping her talking was all I could do. I needed her as much as she needed me. The fire rescue workers tried to do more to help us, but it didn't matter what you did. He was there. It took them a while to find his head. I think at that time, time slowed right down. Everything was in slow motion. It seemed like the more we wanted it over, the longer it took to get things done. It's never a good thing to see someone who has had a part of their body ripped off. I guess it's because we know we can do something to save them if we hurry. But not this. It's so final, and it's the most horrific thing to see."

Sharon was sitting back up with her face down in her hands when she asked, "Were they from here?"

"No, they were from down East. New Brunswick, I believe, is what was on his license."

"Their poor families. What a blow this will be to them all, and being so close to Christmas. Their Christmases will never be the same again. Their lives have all changed in a matter of minutes. Their shock and disbelieve will be hard on them all."

"Yes, Mom. To lose a whole family is more than any one should have to do. To lose someone you love tears you apart inside, but not this. It will be a nightmare for all those involved. It will be a nightmare for us, and I don't think things will be great for us for a while either, Mom."

"Aw, sweetheart, I'm sorry. You're right, of course. I hope you are able to handle it, Jessy, or get the help you will need."

"There is no help other than time, Mom. To talk about it just keeps it alive and fresh in my memory. I would sooner just let it go. So after today, if I don't bring it up, please don't either."

"Just promise that if you feel you need to talk about it, your dad and I are here for you always."

"I know, Mom, and thank you both. Mitch has good ears, so I don't have to go far." That brought a bit of a chuckle and helped lift the spirits, if only for a brief moment.

"Dad, were you and Mom going out?"

"I was taking your mom to supper and then to the movie."

Jessy looked at her watch then back at Peter, saying, "I think you're late."

"There is always tomorrow, sweetheart."

"I'm sorry, Dad."

"You have nothing to be sorry about. I, on the other hand, have." Peter turned to Mitch and put his hand out. Mitch looked at him with a curious look.

"I want to say I'm sorry for thinking you were the cause of my little girl's distress." Shaking Mitch's hand always felt right. As if there was life being transferred between them. It was strange and wasn't a feeling Peter had had many times over his lifetime. He had shaken hands with many, but there was always something when he took Mitch's hand that made him want to hang on. It made him wonder if Jessy had the same feelings the times he had seen them holding hands. He sure hoped so. This man was a keeper for Jessy, and Peter could tell he loved his daughter with his inner core. It would be a strong love. One that would see them through hell and back. He was glad because with their jobs, they were going to need the strength they can pull from each other to get through times like today.

This made Peter relax, knowing there would be someone to take care of his little girl when he was gone. This had been a heavy weight on his shoulders. He was afraid Jessy would be alone when he was gone, and no father wants that for their daughter. She needed a man to lean on even if she thought otherwise. That thought Peter would keep to himself so she wouldn't get all defensive over it and perhaps push Mitch away to prove she would be okay alone.

"I think I will take your mother for a bit to eat before returning her home. Come, Sharon, let's let these two rest if they can."

"Yes, of course. If you need me, dear, call." Sharon kissed Jessy on the cheek as she got up off the sofa. Then, turning, she hugged Mitch. His hugs were strong and sincere as Peter's were. She knew her daughter was in good hands.

Peter shook Mitch's hand, saying, "Again I'm sorry, Mitch."

"Don't be sorry. I'm sure I would have thought the same if the shoe were on the other foot. Everything is fine, sir."

"Good." Peter patted Mitch on the shoulder as he turned to leave." Call us anytime."

"We will. Thank you."

Once they were out of earshot, Sharon said, "I don't think I could eat a thing, Peter. Could we just sit and talk awhile? If you get hungry, I can make us a sandwich."

"You know, that sounds great to me." Peter thought the evening wouldn't be a waste after all.

Sharon was thinking, *Maybe this evening will still work out.* That put a smile on her face as she snuggled into Peter's side.

Chapter 20

Peter and Sharon had a lovely evening in spite of what their daughter and Mitch had been through.

"Peter, if you don't mind, I would love to change."

"I think you look delicious the way you are. Red is your color, dear."

"Thank you, but it won't take me long." She left him sitting on the sofa. She knew he wasn't going anywhere, and she was just going to put the icing on the cake. This was the time the saying "You can't have your cake and eat it too" didn't apply. Peter was having both. Now whether he knew it or not, she didn't care.

Putting on her new red nightie and sleep coat made her feel like a princess in a story. She had lucked out on this one. Beautiful wasn't describing it at all. Being anxious to see what Peter would say, she hurried more than usual, stopping long enough to freshen her perfume and check herself out in the mirror. She had a good hair day for once, so this was easy. When she brought drinks in for her and Peter, as she handed him his all, he could say was, "You're breathtaking, my dear."

"Why, thank you. I know you like the red dress, Peter."

"Say no more. I like this even more. In fact, I love what you have on now. Come sit beside me and let me feel that fabric. I bet it is some smooth under the fingertips."

"Well, I don't know about smooth. You will have to check that out for yourself," Sharon said as she slipped down beside him. Peter wrapping his arms around her made her feel like there was no other place in the whole world she would rather be.

"You know, darling, you make everything you wear look so elegant. I don't know how you do it. I'm sure this would not be so breathtaking on anyone else."

"Now, Peter, don't be so biased."

"Biased? Dear Lord. Lady, can't you see how lovely you truly are?"

"I love that you think that, Peter. You are a very well-put-together man, and I love the true cowboy you really are. Please don't ever change that, okay?"

"No fear in that, my dear. I think this old cowboy is too old to change. So you're stuck with just who I am."

"That is fine with me."

Peter leaned over and kissed Sharon gently. He didn't want to scare her off, and he wanted to be sure to treat her as the lady she was. One thing about Sharon, she never faltered as far as being a true lady. He had told her many times she was wasting her time bookkeeping. She should be teaching young girls how to be ladies. There weren't many ladies walking the street today, and as the new generations take over, he was afraid the word *lady* would no longer be in their vocabulary. He was going to hang on to the one he had, come hell or high water.

The next few days, Peter went into town and he and Sharon made their daily visits to check up on Jessy and Mitch. Jessy had taken this accident very hard and was thinking of maybe getting some professional help. Sleep was not coming easy to her, and when she did fall asleep, she had nightmares.

Mitch had told her he was also having some problems, but he tried to help her as much as he could by sitting and holding Jessy on the sofa until they both would drift off. It would only be for a short time as one of them always woke up in a confused state, Mitch not as much as Jessy. He felt it was the motherly instinct in her that had her more upset than him. Consoling her sometimes took a lot of effort.

When Sharon and Peter would stop over, he would run down to the station and check on things. They had been given time off due to the circumstances. No one there had ever dealt with anything so horrific, so they were all being very understanding and were glad it had not happened on their shift. Many of them felt that they too would be having a hard time with the issue, hoping they never see something like that on their shift. It was something they think about on their way to an accident. How bad is it? What are they going to have to deal with once they are there? Dealing with children who are in the accidents was very hard on most of them, the fact that they are innocent and had no choice but to be there. Depending on someone else for their safety, and they have been let down. A death of anyone is hard, but a child's is always devastating to see.

A family wiped out in the blink of an eye. Like in this case, and the driver of the truck walked away with not a scratch. Mentally he will be scarred for life. Although due to weather and road conditions, he was not to blame. Most of the truck drivers do blame themselves, thinking they should have pulled off the road earlier. After all, they are considered professional drivers. They know long before everyone else what the roads are like. When you take a chance, anything can happen. As the saying goes, hindsight is twenty-twenty.

After three weeks, Jessy had almost gotten her life back. She had gone for professional help. It helped her in many ways. Missing work wasn't something she liked to do. After all, this was her job, and learning to deal with something so horrifying was just another stepping stone to her being able to help someone else. There was no doubt in her mind that she would have to deal with something this bad again. After all, she was young and had many working days and years ahead of her. She hoped this would make her better prepared for the next time. All she could do was pray that there would never be a next time.

Jessy was lucky, and the local paper had gotten hold of a family picture, which even had their dog in it. The picture had been taken at Christmas of last year. She had printed it off to size to fit on the family cross, Laminating it so the weather couldn't damage it. She was able to put. The Beaner Family & Pet on the cross in big bold letters. There was nothing fancy about the cross. She felt it was better than putting a cross up for each of them. They were a family and had died as a family. It was simple, yet it carried a lot of punch to see the faces of the family and their pet that had been wiped out within minutes.

Jessy had said a prayer of thank-you to God for not leaving one on this earth to face all the unknown alone. It is sad when there is a lone survivor. Their world had been torn apart, and to go on alone makes life almost unbearable. Some go on, but they are never whole. Others heal as though nothing had ever happened to them. Guess those were the lucky ones. Those were the ones who have total faith in God and believe in the fact that he had a purpose for how things turned out.

For the others who were not strong believers in the first place, it only made them mad and hate the man who is referred to as God. To them, if there were such a God and a great God as we are raised to believe, he would not have let that happen. The anger in some never dulls, and the pain sits at the surface for their loss for the rest of their lives.

For some of those people, the bottom of the bottle is their only escape. For some, once they have hit the very bottom, they start their slow climb back to the top, not realizing whose hand it is they are holding on to while making their way up that steep hill. He is giving them the strength they need to come back. He had sat off to the side and gave them the time they needed to heal. Everyone heals at a different pace, and when they have decided to live again and climb out of their dark hole, a voice inside their heads will say, "*Take my hand and let me guide you.*"

People have found the strength they need. The courage to move forward. It was something that came easy once they believed. Believing in yourself and a higher power will always see you through.

Jessy believed there was someone or something stronger than all that ran the universe. She was not afraid of it, for she felt it had been with her on many of her trips. Seeing her through whatever it was she was facing.

ROAD SIDE CROSSES

Once she had accepted the fact she could not help any of the family that had just lost their lives, she had prayed for the strength to move on. If that meant by getting professional help, then so be it. When she made that decision, a weight had lifted from her shoulders, and she knew she would be fine. As sad as it was, Jessy now knew she could go forward and do her job as well as she had always done. Jessy and Mitch had fallen back into a pleasant routine.

Christmas was two weeks away Sharon and Peter had gone all out on the decorating the farm inside and out. It looked like a real fantasyland. Peter had so many things in the yard that moved. He said he didn't remember them having these things when Jessy was little. The lights lit the whole farm yard up. It was just so beautiful to see.

Trisha and Crystal were coming for Christmas this year, and this had Sharon and Peter more excited about Christmas than they had ever been. They were all out shopping for that little girl. No one was holding back. From clothes to toys, they had left nothing out.

Mitch was just as guilty as the others. "You know, Jessy, I don't know that little girl, but the way you and Sharon speak of her, I'm sure she must be an angel."

"Oh, she is an angel. She is the prettiest little girl I have ever seen." Jessy had shown Mitch the pictures Trisha had sent to her over the months. They were all stuck on her fridge. In fact, her fridge looked like it was a scrapbook. Jessy had done a neat job on her fridge. It was all about that little girl.

Sharon, on the other hand, had one big picture and a few smaller ones sitting out. All the others were in her grandma's brag book that she carried around in her purse. She and Peter flipped through it often, admiring how the sweet little girl had grown and changed in such a short time. It had been many years since they had anything to do with a child. So everything Crystal did was remarkable in their eyes.

"Do you think she will go see her parents while they are here?" Mitch asked.

"No, Mitch, I don't think so. Trisha likes to stay as far away from them as possible."

"She won't even want to take the little girl over to meet her grandparents?"

"She said no."

"That is pretty sad, don't you think?"

"Mitch, you have to understand. Her parents are drunk all the time, and they fight nonstop. Who would want to take a child into that?"

"Couldn't she arrange for them to have a short half-hour visit? Tell them they have to be on their best behavior if they want to see their grandchild."

"I suppose she could try, but it's not our call. Remember, Trisha is the one that grew up in that most of her life. She didn't come and live with us until she was old enough to make her own decision. God, when I think about it, if Mom and Dad hadn't taken her in, she could have ended up on the street."

"Where did she go when your parents divorced?"

"She moved in with a friend of hers from school. They got their own place. Mom and Dad helped her even then. Although they separated, they never let it interfere with what Trisha or I needed. They were great with us. I had always thought Trisha and I would become roommates in college, but she never stayed here. She was so embarrassed by her parents she got out as soon as an opportunity presented itself. She came back to visit us every chance she got until she made more friends, then we didn't see much of her. She and I called back and forth and tried to keep things tight between us. That dwindled off, and it was quite a while before I knew why. I was worried that I had finally lost the only other person that I had ever considered family besides my mom and dad. My best friend, my sister."

Chapter 21

"Why was that? Was she mad at your parents?"

"No, she was pregnant and didn't know how to tell them. She thought it would really hurt them when they found out. After all they had done for her and the fact they believed in her. She felt she had let them down. I was surprised how well they took it when I told them about the baby. Of course, I didn't say anything until she had had the baby."

"A bit of a coward, were you?"

"Guess in some ways I felt the same as Trisha. I thought that if by chance she were to lose it, then they would never have had to know. Once she had Crystal, there was no more hiding it."

"You think your parents would be okay with you having a baby out of wedlock?"

"Me!"

"Yeah, you. Do you think they would accept it as easy as they did with Trisha?"

"One thing is for sure, I wouldn't be able to wait until the baby was born to tell them."

Mitch chuckled with that thought. "That wasn't an answer, Jessy."

"Today I would think so. A few years ago, they would have been very upset with me. I think they are so ready to be grandparents that it wouldn't even matter what color or how many I would have. Look at how they have gone all out for Crystal for Christmas. She is so young she won't even remember this Christmas."

"You had better take lots of pictures so you can talk to her about it all the time she is growing up."

"We will have to send some home with Trisha so she too can show her and talk to her about it. Guess that would be one way of her remembering this Christmas."

"I believe in the fact that if someone talks to you enough about something, you finally think you do remember. Maybe that would be a good thing for Crystal. To know she spent her first Christmas surrounded by all the people who love her."

"That's sweet of you to say that, and it's true."

"Yeah, it is." Surprising Jessy, he pulled her in and kissed her like he had never done before.

There was something moving about the kiss that rattled Jessy. She didn't know if she should push him away or hold on for all she was worth. Her heart felt like it would jump out of her chest. His kisses were always light, like a friend would kiss a friend. Nothing serious, just a kind gesture of affection. All friends had this. It was acceptable among friends. You just kissed your friends lightly on the lips or cheeks like almost in passing. Not loaded with passion as this one was. Where was Mitch coming from? Where did he think this would go?

"Oh gosh. I'm sorry, Jessy. What was I thinking? Guess all this family-love talk got to me. I'm really sorry."

"Don't worry about it. No harm done. At least we know we are still alive when it comes to kissing. After all, neither one of us has been dating. Maybe a practice run once in a while doesn't hurt anything."

That lightened the mood, but Mitch was embarrassed that he had let it go that far. If he was honest with himself, he would have to admit he had wanted to do that for a very long time. He also knew one didn't mix work with relationships. To have one, you have to let the other one go. He knew neither he nor Jessy were ready to do that. Besides, after all this time, what would he do? What would she do? They both loved their work. He had stepped over the line. It was a dangerous line to step over and one there was no turning back from.

The days ahead went as usual, and the kiss never interfered in their lives. In one way, Mitch was taken aback by it. He had thought that he had become important to Jessy. But if the kiss didn't affect her, then it was obvious that they had just a working relationship and there would never be anything else. This weighed heavy on Mitch's heart. He had hoped she was the one. Jessy was so down-to-earth and so kind and very interesting to talk to, and she was fun to be with. Best of all, she didn't need a man. She was independent, and she would be a great wife for someone. He loved the fact that Jessy could hold her own in any situation and get by with the odd shoulder to lean on from time to time. Jessy was a very strong woman, and he loved her for it.

He had a problem with women who were in total need of a man. He based it all on being lazy. Mitch knew there was a difference between women who stayed home and took care of the kids and house. The ones he had a problem with were the ones who did nothing all day and still couldn't keep the house clean. He had friends who lived like that, and he just shook his head. What man in his right mind would keep a woman where he worked long hours then had to clean house and make meals and tend to the kids when he got home?

He also had friends that were at the opposite end of that scale, and that was where he would want to be. He would want to come home to everything clean and meals at least started and the kids clean and tended to. That would make him happy. Mitch knew he would pitch in and help once he was home. Having to was another story. He knew he wanted to be a hands-on type of father and husband. He also knew things never worked out as you plan. Love works in mysterious ways. Perhaps there is no one out there for him. After all, he had not even been interested.

Jessy had awakened those feelings in him, and he knew deep down if he couldn't make him and Jessy a couple, then he would be single for the rest of his life. Having Jessy as a friend, a very good friend, was great too. So long as she didn't bring another man into the picture. Mitch knew that would destroy him, and he would put in for a transfer. It would tear his heart apart to see her give hers to someone else. Mitch had known for quite a while now that his heart belonged to Jessy. He didn't know what he was going to do about it. They had talked about their dreams of the future. Marriage and family were never mentioned. He had no idea why not. He did know he would bring it up someday soon and see what Jessy had to say.

He knew couples who had both, and he figured someday he would like to try it. After all, he wasn't getting any younger.

"Hey, Mitch, are we going Christmas shopping after work today?"

"You mean you haven't bought the store all out yet?"

"Hell, no. I'm just getting started. After all, it only comes once a year."

"It's a good thing, Jessy. You would be in the poor house."

She laughed as she refilled what was missing from her medic bag. They had had a call for a woman who was delivering her baby at home then she panicked and decided she needed more help than the midwife. Jessy and Mitch were there to see the birth of her son and then took them to the hospital.

Mom and baby were both strong and healthy. They would be sent home the next day.

"Just think of the fun that new mother was going to have shopping this close to Christmas for her son," Jessy said.

"Hope she's not like you and buying out the stores."

"Now, Mitch, don't be such a scrooge."

"Scrooge, never, but I do think there should be a limit."

"Limit. Yeah, you're probably right. Everyone else can worry about the limit. I'm going to spoil Crystal this year."

"You and your folks."

"We have never had a little one to spoil for Christmas. It is going to be a blast watching Crystal with her gifts this year."

"You do know as she gets older, it will be more expensive and you won't be able to get her so much."

"Guess we will deal with that then. Right now, I'm going to enjoy spoiling her."

"Be careful. You will make her expect too much for Christmas instead of appreciating what she has gotten."

Going over to Mitch and placing a light kiss on his cheek, Jessy said, "Now, Mitch, don't be all humbug and spoil my fun. This is our first Christmas with Trisha in a long time and our first that is going to have excitement with a child, and that is what Christmas is all about. You have to admit this has been more exciting than the last two Christmases. It's only been us old people that sleep till noon on Christmas Day. Mom always said Christmas was for children."

"She does, does she?" Smiling, Mitch put his arms lightly around Jessy's waist and pulled her in for a hug. He planted a kiss on the top of her head.

"Kids and Christmas, you say? Guess we will have to see what we can do about that."

"Yes, and every year, Mom spends big bucks buying toys for the Christmas hamper then she volunteers on the wrapping end. Mom always said she wished she could be the one to do the drop-offs. She would like to see the faces of the children, along with the faces of the parents as miracles have been brought to their door, and in the end, they have a merry Christmas."

"Your mom loves Christmas. I can see where you get all your Christmas spirit from."

"No, Mom is Christmas."

Chapter 22

Mitch and Jessy had taken a run into the bigger center after work. Mitch was looking for something special. He never did say what. Mitch was very adamant that he had to go that day.

A trip to the bigger center wasn't Jessy's favorite thing to do. Jessy liked to shop in all the little shops around home. They were so full of Christmas spirit. It was always like a blast of ancient history would come to life on their streets in town. Most of the stores had the decorations from when they first opened. Ones you couldn't buy today. They were nostalgic and simply Christmas.

The town decorated the streets, making them look like a picture-perfect Christmas card no matter which end you looked at it from. The heavy snow would add the glitter. Some of the neighbors would use their horse and sleighs at this time of year just to bring back the feeling of Christmas past. It was the most spectacular time of year.

The huge tree that grew at the center of the town square was always perfectly done with lights. There were always parcels put under that tree for the homeless' Christmas Eve. The parcels consist of anything a man or woman could use for the winter. The homeless were as one big family and would all gather there and pass out the parcels, exchanging their item with whoever needed it. They made sure everyone had a parcel to open.

There had never been a bad incident accrue, so the townspeople carried on their tradition of helping the poor. It had been going on since Jessy could remember. The town hall always had a big turkey dinner for those folks who wished to celebrate and be out of the cold for the day. Jessy had often helped out there with Sharon and Peter. To them, that was what Christmas was all about.

Jessy had lucked out and found the perfect picture frame for her mom. It read, *"All those who touch your heart are your family."* Jessy was thinking of Trisha and Crystal. She would make sure her mom had the perfect picture of them to put in it.

When she came out of the shop, she saw Mitch going toward a bench with two cups and a bag in his hands. He then handed one of the cups and the bag to the old man sitting on the bench. Jessy figured by the look of him he was a homeless man. Mitch must have bought him something to eat. She could tell that Mitch and him were having a serious conversation, and she didn't know if she should interfere, so she just hung back to see what Mitch was going to do.

A couple times she saw Mitch put his hand on the old man's shoulder, and the then the old man would shake his head in agreement. She figured Mitch was giving him a lecture on eating and taking care of himself. Jessy figured Mitch had listened to her and her parents talk about helping the homeless this time of year, and it had worn off on him.

ROAD SIDE CROSSES

Watching as Mitch pulled his wallet out and took what seemed like a fair amount of money out, giving it to the old man, smiling all the time he was doing it, Jessy's heart melted on the spot. What a kind thing for Mitch to do for the old man this close to Christmas. The two men got up, and although he looked like a big man, he was stooped over. They had attempted a hug and a handshake at the same time, which put a smile on Jessy's face. Most men were uncomfortable when it came to hugging another man.

The handshake was a slow-release one. This was something she had noticed with Mitch and his handshakes, He never just shook and dropped his hand. It always looked like he enjoyed his handshakes. That too warmed Jessy's heart. Mitch wasn't afraid to be seen holding another man's hand. He was a very kind soul, and he would never hurt anyone. Mitch was a big man with an even bigger heart.

Thinking to herself, *That's one of the things I love about him.*

Mitch spotted Jessy then she noticed he was saying farewell to the old fella. Before she knew it, Mitch was at her side.

"Did you find what you were looking for, Mitch?"

"Yes, I did."

Jessy looked at him strangely as he didn't have any packages in hand. So what was it that he had found?

"How about you, what did you find?"

"The perfect picture frame for Mom."

"Ready to go for supper before we go home?"

"Yes, I am hungry."

"Okay. I know this great place just down around the corner."

"Great. Let's eat."

The restaurant was just as good as Mitch had said it was. Decorated for Christmas with Christmas songs playing softly in the background and the fireplace glowing made a person feel like you could sit there all night. Having a glass a wine beside the fire before going home, Jessy decided to ask about the old man.

"It was nice of you to help that old man, Mitch."

"Oh, I didn't help him with anything. He is too proud to take help, and besides that, he really doesn't need help. Not that way."

"Where was he from?"

"Here." It was like Mitch didn't want to talk about the old man.

Jessy pushed a little more. "Was he going anywhere for Christmas?"

"I don't think so. He hasn't for a long time. Christmas comes and goes, and he usually stays hidden away at this time of year." With that said, Jessy saw sadness wash over Mitch's eyes.

"Mitch, what's wrong?" she asked, reaching over and placing a hand upon his arm.

"Nothing's wrong, Jess."

"Then why do you look so sad? Who was the old man? Did you know him?"

Mitch hung his head for a few seconds before looking back up at Jessy. "Yeah, Jess, I know him. It is my dad."

Jessy's mouth dropped as she said, "Your dad? Mitch, why didn't you introduce me to him? I would have loved to have met him. Did you ask him to come to Dad's for Christmas?"

"No, Jessy, I did not ask him."

"Mitch, it's Christmas."

"Yes, and that's why I didn't."

"I don't understand. Don't you want to be with him on Christmas?"

"Nothing I would like more, Jess, but that will never happen."

"That is so sad, Mitch. How come? Is he a Jehovah's Witness?"

That brought a chuckle from Mitch, and he shook his head. "No. My dad is a lot of things, but religious he is not. He says there is a God, but nowhere does it say you have to go to church. You are just to rest on Sunday and be kind to everyone. You should treat everyone as though they are your family."

"He sounds like a smart man, one I would like to know."

"He was a smart man at one time."

"Then what happened?"

"When Mom died, so did my dad. My whole life changed from that day on."

"I'm sorry, Mitch."

"Don't be sorry. It is what it is."

Jessy couldn't help but hear the deep sorrow in Mitch's voice. "It's been a long time since your mom died, Mitch. What does your dad do now?"

"Not a damn thing."

"Is he a drunk now?"

"No, he never turned to the bottle. He just slipped into depression, and that's where he will die."

"You don't think if he were to be asked, he would come for Christmas? We could always come and get him."

Mitch hung his head as if he were thinking it over. When he looked up, Jessy could see a tear in the corner of his eye. "Jessy, Mom died Christmas Eve."

Dropping her wineglass brought the waitress over immediately. "May I help you?"

Jessy now had turned red in the face. She was embarrassed and was shocked. "I'm so sorry."

"It's okay, miss, it happens all the time."

Jessy wanted to say, "I don't think so." She was watching Mitch and wasn't really sure what to say. They sat in silence as the waitress cleaned up the glass.

"Thank you."

"No problem, miss. May I get you another glass?"

"No, I think I'm fine. Thank you." All this time, she kept her eyes on Mitch. If she only knew what he was thinking right now. What was she to say?

"Jessy, I'm fine. I just wish dad was able to move on."

"Your mom and dad were close."

"In their own way. Nothing like your mom and dad. Yet they loved each other. Dad has a hard time showing his affection, but Mom knew he loved her. She never wanted for anything. Mom was very easily pleased, and she liked the simple life. Fancy was not Mom either. Mom was a very pretty woman like your mom. Except she was more the jeans-and-sweater kind of woman, always looked nice. Even when she was so sick, she tried so hard to keep up her appearances for Dad. The day her hair started to fall out was a hard day for Mom. She cried for many days. Dad tried to tell her that it didn't matter, it would grow back, she was still beautiful to us."

"Did it grow back like she wanted it to?"

"No, she had passed away before it could."

"Oh, Mitch, I'm so sorry you have had to go through that. It scares me to think about losing Mom and Dad. I know everything will change the day I lose one of them."

"You don't realize just how right you are, Jessy. Knowing there is nothing you can do for them or to stop the changes that are going to happen. I stayed with my dad for the first year. The doctors had said the first year would be hard but things would get better after that, so I stayed. After six months, I had almost gone crazy and dad wasn't talking to anyone. I was told to talk about our lives with Mom and that would help him, but it only made him angry, and he sunk further into depression. So I quit bringing Mom's name up to him, and after a while, it was like I had never had a mother. Dad had gone through the house one day shortly after Mom had died. He was very angry, and he took all the Christmas decorations down and burned them. He said there would never be another Christmas so long as he lived."

"Why was he so mad about Christmas? That's not what killed her."

"He knows that. It's one thing that Mom loved, maybe not as much as Sharon, but Mom loved Christmas. Mom's best part about Christmas was Christmas Eve and going to midnight mass. She loved to sing the old Christmas carols. She had passed away listening to them. I always felt that God took her home on the Eve that meant so much to her. I thought it was very appropriate. Dad didn't see it that way. When Dad sold the house and his business then moved into his tiny apartment, I moved on. I went back once a week at first. Then it stretched out to a month then six months. He wouldn't talk to me, and it hurt so bad because I had lost both my parents and had no one to talk to. It was hard not going back to see him. I felt it must hurt him not seeing me. I never wanted him to think I quit loving him, but I wasn't strong enough to do it anymore."

"How often do you see him now?"

"Those days I would tell you I had to go out of town, I was going over to see Dad."

"He seemed like he liked talking to you. You were chatting up quite a storm when I saw you."

"I do most of the talking, but he will answer me now, so we are moving ahead slowly."

Chapter 23

"Aw, Mitch, that is good, but it's still sad about Christmas and that he will be alone."

"Well, that is how Mr. Ed Acorn wishes it to be. I have learned over the years not to fight him on it. It only made things worse for us. I don't buy gifts for him. I just give him money. That way, he can spend it on whatever he wants. My dad doesn't need my money, and at first, he wouldn't take it. I would just leave it on his table when I left. I wanted him to know I still loved him and I care and I would give him Christmas if he would just let me. He did tell me Merry Christmas this time."

"Oh, Mitch, that is great. See, he will come around. You will have Christmas with your dad again someday."

"Maybe. In the meantime, it is what it is."

"Mitch, does it bother you to be with my family for Christmas Eve? I will understand if you wish to spend it alone with your memories."

"No, I love it. I know Mom would want me to be enjoying Christmas as we once did. You don't do things the same way, so it doesn't bring pain, only happiness."

"We have never gone to church for Christmas Eve mass. What's it like?"

"It was always something that made me feel right. I don't know how to explain it. Like God knew I was paying him a visit and everything would be all right after that. I guess it was like letting him know I didn't forget about his loss and to show him I was grateful. It always brings tears, yet I'm happy. Go figure."

"We will have to try for no tears this year, Mitch. With Trisha and Crystal coming, there won't be time for tears."

"You're right, Jessy. We have much to be happy for."

"Yes, we do."

"I think it's time to head for home."

"I think so too."

They hadn't any bags other than the one Jessy had with the picture frame in it, so their packing was fast. Which brought her around to asking Mitch about his shopping. "Mitch, what did you really come for tonight?"

"To meet my dad. I wanted to give him some money for Christmas, and he said he would meet me for coffee. He didn't know about the money. He just wanted coffee. So I thought I would do it at the same time."

"That was sweet of you."

"He doesn't drive far anymore, so for him to come see me, I could be waiting a very long time. He won't sit long and talk, so this works for us. He says he just wants to see me so he knows I'm okay. We keep it short because I don't think he is ever going to be up to any real conversations. I think he is scared it would end up being about Mom. It's not a road he wants to walk. So I will keep it simple and short until he tells me or shows me otherwise."

"You're a good son, Mitch. I'm sure your dad loves you, and he knows you love him."

"I never doubted that for a moment."

"I hope neither of you ever have that doubt. I watched Trisha go through that most of her life. It is a horrible thing to think you are not loved by the ones who should love you the most."

"Trisha's parents love her. Just in a different way is all."

"You really believe that, Mitch?"

"Yes, I do. I can't see there being a parent out there that wouldn't love their child. They just can't handle being a parent, but to love is easy."

"I don't believe love is easy, Mitch."

"How hard can it be to love a child, Jessy? I see the children of my friends, and they are cute, funny, and full of energy. They are able to melt anyone's heart, so yes, I think it would be easy to love a child. I think some parents have a problem with responsibility. Thinking that children should be able to take care of themselves, which mean they themselves have not matured enough to take that responsibility on. In some cases, the child ends up taking care of the parents."

"I don't understand how Trisha made it to the age she was before she moved in with us. How as a baby did she survive?"

"Her parents obviously loved her enough to take care of her up until then. Perhaps they didn't do it the same way as your parents or others would have, but that doesn't mean they didn't love her."

"You have a good point, Mitch. Perhaps you should talk to Trisha when she comes home for Christmas. I know my mom and dad have talked to her, but I don't think they see it your way, but it might help Trisha a lot."

"If the time presents itself, I might just do that. I won't go out of my way and stick my nose in, but if the conversation comes up, I will say how I feel about it. If it helps her great. I feel bad that her parents don't get to see their grandchild."

"That bothers me as well. I can't see myself ever keeping Mom and Dad from seeing their grandchildren."

"Grandchildren. How many do you want?"

"I don't really know. I've never thought too much about it. Maybe four."

"Me too. I think that would be a good number."

"Three is an odd number, and I think one would always be left out."

This was the first time Mitch and Jessy had ever talked about having a family. At one time, Jessy would not have even continued the conversation, but now it seemed right. She thought she must be getting mellow in her old age. She found she could talk to Mitch about anything without feeling pressured one way or the other. That was why she thought of him as her very best friend.

"Oh my, what do we have up there?" They could see lights from police cars. It looked to be serious, so Mitch pulled off to the side of the road, and he and Jessy ran up to the cars to see what was going on.

It was a car of teenagers on their way back home. The driver had lost control. No one knew how serious their injuries were yet. Mitch and Jessy told them who they were and asked if they could help. They were told their help would be appreciated, so Mitch ran back to his truck and grabbed his medic bag. He was like Jessy and never left home without it.

"Jessy, let's tend to the one lying over in the snow."

"I'm right behind you, Mitch."

The snow was up past their knees, and so going wasn't easy. They found it was a young man of about sixteen or seventeen.

"He must not have been wearing his seat belt. He is lucky not to be under the car."

"You're probably right, Jess. God, it only takes seconds to put it on."

"Mind you, I don't think the ones in the car are any better off right now."

"It's a small car. Not much room for mistakes."

The moaning from the young man was a good sign. At least there was still life.

"Son, can you hear me?" Mitch asked.

The young man moaned again.

"My partner and I are going to help you, so please just stay calm, okay?"

He was bleeding heavily from his head, probably from going through the windshield. There was blood coming from his mouth, which wasn't a good sign, perhaps a punctured lung. Mitch was sure he had a broken leg. It was lying in a strange position that if it wasn't broken there was no way it would be like that. He would wait to get a board before moving the leg. It would be painful, so Mitch didn't want to move him more than once.

Jessy started to wrap his head as Mitch checked for more cuts and broken bones. Jessy wanted to stop the bleeding as much as she could. They did all they could do for the young man, and Jessy stayed with him while Mitch went back up to the car to see if he could get a board so they could get the young man out of the snow. By now there were other people who had stopped, and the ambulances had arrived.

They were arranging to have some of the men gathered and were telling them they would have to lift the car. One of the teens had not been so lucky and was trapped under the car. It was a good thing the car was small, and they figured the men who were there could lift it easy enough. All the teens in the car had been removed. They only had the two outside left to load in the ambulance.

As the men lifted the car, Mitch and one other medic were able to get to the teen. It was a female, and she was facedown. Checking her for a pulse, Mitch discovered that the young girl was dead. They hoped strongly that she would be the only death victim of this accident.

While Mitch was helping with the car, Jessy had helped another paramedic get the young boy brought up to the ambulance. When all was done, they found out that they had more teens in the car than seat belts.

It was going to be a sad Christmas for these teens who had lost one of their friends, and perhaps they would lose another before the night was through.

Jessy had found out when she had talked to the one teen that the ones lying outside the car were brother and sister. They were the last ones to be picked up. They were all going into the bigger center to take in a new movie that had just been released. It would be horrible for that family to lose both their children, and this close to Christmas. Winter can be the most beautiful time of year yet the deadliest.

"Where the hell were the parents of those teens? Did they not know there wasn't room for their children to be traveling safely?"

"Teens do a lot of sneaky things, Jess. Their parents might not have even known they were going."

"Oh God, Mitch. That will be a shock to hear that their daughter is dead, and perhaps their son won't make it through the night."

"It's a parents' worst nightmare come true."

"On second thought, I don't want to have children. I can't imagine what that must do to you as a parent."

"Do you think it's different from losing a parent, Jess?"

"Yes, I do. Especially so young. I would think as a parent you would blame yourself all the time. The guilt of knowing you could have prevented it. Once we become adults out on our own, it's different. We then have control of our lives, and it's up to us to see that we are safe. But while you're a child under your parents' care, it is up to them to see to your safety."

"Jess, you can't prevent everything that might happen to a child while growing up. Just think about it. Were your parents with you 24-7? No one could expect that, so you can't prevent all terrible accidents from happening."

"I suppose you're right, but I can't help but hurt for those parents tonight."

"Of course you can't. I feel the same way. I can't imagine answering that door tonight. It was only a couple hours ago they saw their son and daughter happy, going out with friends. Tomorrow will be like they never knew the life before the accident. It may even destroy them. By the age of those teens, I would think that was their whole family in that car tonight."

"Oh, Mitch, what can we do?"

"Nothing. Not a damn thing, Jess. We did what we could do for them already tonight. We have to pray that the boy will pull through. Losing one is hard enough."

"Yeah, I guess you're right. Sure makes a person feel helpless."

Mitch reached over and puts his hand on top of Jessy's hand. "You have to remember, Jess, we are not God. We took the training for helping those victims. We did our best tonight, and the rest is up to him and them. You know that."

Chapter 24

Mitch and Jessy rode in silence for the rest of their trip. Both were engaged in their own thoughts. Every now and again, they would see a house off in the distance decorated for Christmas that they would comment on, but that was it as far as conversation went. It was strange how some of the accidents would affect them more than another. Jessy knew that if it had happened at home, she would have gone home in silence, and somehow she felt Mitch would have done the same. They mourn the loss of a life no matter whose it was. It was just a natural feeling to have. Death, no matter whose it is, is sad. No one said you had to know the person to grieve for them. Grieving is a way of life and a human thing to do. After all, they were someone's husband, wife, mother, father, grandparent. In this case, it was someone's child.

Jessy would not be making a cross for the young girl. She only hoped that someone would. It was out of her district, so she would just leave it be.

After Mitch had dropped her off, she called Sharon to let her know they were back and about the accident. Jessy didn't have to call Peter. He was with Sharon, so she only had to go over the details once.

She would wait to tell them about Mitch's dad when she saw them. Although there wasn't much to tell, she found herself wishing at that moment they too could meet his dad. By what Mitch had said about him, she figured they would like him. Besides, Mitch was his son, and they all loved him very much.

Mitch had a shower and had thought about going over to see Jessy. Taking a beer and sitting in his chair thinking over the events of the day, he decided he would just stay put.

His dad was playing heavy on his mind although he knew he was well and he did seem to be happier this time than he had been for many years. Christmas was just around the corner, and he would miss his dad on Christmas Day. Thinking that, just maybe he should skip going to Peter's and go back over and spend the day with his dad. What could it hurt? After all, Trisha and Crystal would be at Peter's, and he didn't want to intrude on a family dinner.

It had been almost twenty-five years since his mom passed away, and this was the first time his dad had shown any signs of life.

He was feeling foolish now. Why hadn't he talked to his dad about it tonight? Was it because he was afraid it was short lived, or was it because he didn't believe what he was seeing? His dad had actually smiled at him while they were talking, and then to wish him Merry Christmas had almost left Mitch speechless. Maybe after all these years, Mitch would have a merry Christmas. Perhaps he could make sure his dad did as well. He would give it more thought, and when he felt the time was right, he would let Jessy know he was going to go spend Christmas with his dad.

With that decision made, Mitch drifted off to sleep in his big chair and slept soundly until 5:30 a.m.

Jessy never slept much at all. She had worried about the family of those teens part of the night. It was about 1 a.m. when she decided to do some Christmas wrapping. Putting on Christmas music and getting into wrapping finally took her mind off the tragedy.

Waking up, she felt like she could take on the world with what little sleep she got. She was sad for those who were suffering their loss right now, but she was also excited about Christmas. Just the idea that there would be a toddler running loose in the house Christmas morning put a whole different meaning to Christmas. She thought, *So this is what Christmas is supposed to feel like. This is what is known as having the Christmas spirit.* She was giddy and happy this morning in spite of herself and what had taken place the night before.

Her mom and dad were coming over today after work, and that had her happy as well, in a different kind of way. She loved to see them together every chance she could. Yes, Christmas was going to be great. She would have all the ones who meant the most to her with her. What more could she ask for?

The weather had warmed up a little, and it made roads and sidewalks a little slippery. The snow banks were high, and paths had been shoveled between stores to be able to cross the streets. It was hard for some of the seniors to walk. Most of the younger people took their time and made sure to help the seniors who were having trouble. After all, we will all be there someday, and we can only hope that we will get the help that we will be needing.

When she got into work, she found Mitch had brought coffee in and some doughnuts. "What's this? We don't go out for coffee this morning?"

"We will. I was just up early and was bored, so you get spoiled this morning. Your coffee may even be cold."

"I like cold coffees."

Just then a call came in.

"Looks like it's a good thing I grabbed us some," Mitch said as he held his cup up high.

"For sure," Jessy said as she grabbed her coffee, and they ran for their unit.

When they got to their location, they had found an older couple were doing Christmas shopping and the woman slipped getting into the car and cracked her head on the sidewalk. She was unconscious. Her husband was totally beside himself, blaming himself because he didn't have a hold of her arm tight enough to prevent her from falling.

At the hospital, they gave him a sedative to calm him down while his wife was being prepared to be lifted out to the city. Head trauma wasn't something they dealt with in a small place. Mitch and Jessy stayed with Mr. Brooks until his wife was taken away. He had no idea what to do. His son lived five hours away. Jessy got his son's number, and she called him. He said he would meet his father at the hospital. Mr. Brooks couldn't leave on his own.

"Who will take you to the city?" Jessy asked.

"I have a younger brother that lives here. He will take me."

"How about if we take you to your brother's place now?"

"You would do that?"

"Yes, sir, we will. You can't be driving, and you can't stay here. Let's get the information on where they sent your wife so you will know where you're going. Then we will take you to your brother's."

Helping him off the bed was a chore as he was very lightheaded and seemed to be very unstable. Jessy knew some of it was because he was also traumatized with what had happened to his wife. It doesn't take much to throw elderly people off course. It made her want to hold him close and be his strength.

With Mitch on one side and Jessy on the other, they finally got Mr. Brooks into their unit. That was a great thing about living in a small community. They got to help everyone. As it turned out, Mr. Brook's brother lived only minutes away from the hospital, so it didn't tie them up long. He was so grateful for their help he thought he should be paying them for the ride. The poor man was so worried about his wife he couldn't keep his mind on anything that was being said. He didn't understand why she wouldn't wake up and talk to him.

"Betty didn't say good-bye."

"Just remember, she heard you and she knows you love her, and you will see her in a little while."

"Yes, yes."

"You take care, Mr. Brooks. We must go now. We hope you and your wife have a merry Christmas."

"Same to you, dear. Thank you."

When Mitch and Jessy were back in their unit, Mitch asked, "Do you think the old girl will be okay?"

"Hard call. Guess it depends on what kind of damage was sustained from the blow."

"They are fragile at their age. It's like we go back in time after a certain age."

"I have noticed that too. Some hold on to good health and strong bones into their late eighties. Then there are others by the time they are in their sixties, they're old."

"I guess it's all about how you live while you're young."

"Being active all your life, I'm sure, is better."

"Then you should be a strong old woman!"

They were both laughing as they pulled into the station. The rest of the day was quiet, and it went by quickly as Mitch and Jessy got right into doing some extra cleaning around the station. They had hung Christmas decorations around, but now the crew was putting up their Christmas tree the next day and having their own little Christmas party on Saturday. It wasn't much, but they were all family, and it was important to them to show it. It was always fun. They had done what was called a Chinese gift exchange.

"Jess did I hear you say your parents are coming over tonight?" Mitch asked.

"Yes, they are. You coming over?"

"I would love to. Thank you. I will bring the wine."

"You better bring some beer. Dad drank the last one, and he's not much into wine. He says it's a woman's drink."

"I agree, although I have had some great-tasting wine."

"Me too. I don't know how they can drink the dry bitter crap. I like mine sweet."

"Everything about you is sweet."

"Why, thank you, Mitch. I happen to think you're sweet as well. You know I'm looking forward to the Christmas break. Not that I don't like my job. With Trisha coming, I'm glad our days off fall then. We can get caught up with our visiting without me worrying about going to bed because I have to work in the morning or worse be on nights. What about you? Do you plan to spend more time at the farm?"

Mitch wondered if now would be a good time to tell Jessy of his plans to spend time with his dad. He knew if anyone would understand, it would be Jessy. "You know, Jess, I'm not sure what I want to do."

This had Jessy looking at him with a frown. "What do you mean? You are coming to the farm for Christmas morning, aren't you?"

"I'm not sure, Jess."

"Mitch, I thought you were okay with all of this. I don't want to see you sitting alone for Christmas, even Christmas Eve. You're welcome anytime. Mom and Dad love having you around."

"I know that, Jess, but I was thinking I might go over and spend the day with my dad."

Jessy stumbled as she was getting down off a stool. "Mitch, for real. You want to go to your dad's?"

"Yeah, I would like to."

She went over to him and took him into a bear hug.

"You going to bring him here?"

"No, Jess, not this time. I think that would be asking too much. I would like to spend it alone with dad the first time and see how it goes."

"Of course. I understand, Mitch. I think that's great, and I hope it turns out to be the best ever."

Kissing Jessy on top of the head, he said, "Thanks, Jess. I knew you would understand."

"Of course I do. If the shoe was on the other foot, I would be doing the same thing. I'm happy for you, Mitch, and I hope one day we can meet your dad and perhaps have Christmas with him."

"That would be great, Jess. Thanks."

"No problem." Although Jessy was happy for Mitch, she was also sad to know that they wouldn't be spending Christmas together. She also knew her mom and dad would be disappointed, yet they would feel the same as she did. It will be great for Mitch and his dad, after all these years. They will have Trisha and Crystal spending Christmas with them. It was like both families were starting over new.

Chapter 25

The day went by so fast no one knew where the time had gone. Mitch was at Jessy's before Peter and Sharon showed up. The beer was cooling, and wine was on ice. Jessy's apartment was decorated for Christmas, and it was done in red and white. She had been very picky about what she had put up, and although she bought at the dollar store, you couldn't tell. It was all in the way she had put it together. She put heavy greens over her mantel the same as her mom always does. For some reason, that made it feel more like Christmas. It put a real Christmas touch to the home. Jessy used a lot of candles in jars, and it made for a very romantic setting.

"You know, Jess, this is the perfect setting to be proposed to if that was something that was going to happen."

"Well, thank you!" She was blushing, and she knew it. It was a good thing they were in candlelight as it didn't show so easily, but she felt very flushed and had hoped he didn't take it to be a setup.

"Christmas is always romantic, Mitch, no matter how you look at it. It is the most beautiful time of year, and beauty is romantic."

Looking at her beauty, all he could say was, "You're so right."

The doorbell ringing broke the uneasiness between them. They never had that happen before. Everything was so easy with them it always seemed so natural.

The four of them enjoyed a beautiful fun-filled evening. Jessy had so much food put out no one was going hungry. She did confess that the only hard work she had done was take it all out of the boxes. The deli and bakeshop had done the rest.

"You know, Jessy, you are starting to take on some of your mother's traits. You would think she had decorated your apartment for you."

"Thank you, Dad. I know I have a long way to go to do it the same as Mom. I do think it looks very pretty."

"Now, darling, you don't want to do it the same as me. You have to do it your own way, make it special for you. Your taste and your touch, it has to be personal."

"I want to be able to pass the traditions down, Mom, that we have had all these years."

"Some of them are fine, and they seem to get passed down automatically, and others you make. Each family should have their own traditions as well as keep some of the old to pass down. I too think your place is lovely. It is so warm and romantic."

Jessy thought, *Geez, there's that word again.*

Peter caught that right away. Romantic, yes. What the hell had he been thinking? His brain went into overtime. He knew just how he was getting Sharon to move back home. He couldn't believe it was so simple and that he hadn't thought of it before now. Tomorrow couldn't come fast enough. He had big plans to make, and if they didn't win his wife back, he would be screwed. Maybe he should talk to Jessy first to see what she thought. Then he thought no, he wouldn't want her hurt if his plans didn't turn out. This way, he would be the only one who would know, the only one who would be hurt.

The four of them played cards and had a great time. Peter had gotten almost girl giddy as all he could think of was tomorrow. He knew he wouldn't be sleeping tonight. Christmas was in three days, so he had to work fast. He knew Jessy and Mitch were going to their Christmas party the next evening, so they wouldn't be in his way. He just had to be careful not to run into Sharon. They had spent every day together for the last month, so giving her the cold shoulder, so to of speak, may not be that easy. He didn't want to hurt her or upset her this close to Christmas, but in the end, she would understand.

Trisha and Crystal would be in tomorrow, and that would have all the girls in town. There was no doubt they would be asking him to hang out with them. This might be the best time for him to take a trip out of town. There would be no way of running into Sharon and the girls.

Peter was right. There wasn't much sleep for him. He was up and out of town before Sharon got worried and called him.

"Good morning, dear. Were you not coming for breakfast this morning?"

"I'm sorry, Sharon, I'm out of town at the moment. I'm sorry I'd forgotten to tell you last night that I had promised to run old Jack to his daughters."

"That was nice of you, Peter. Okay, we will see you when you get back. Please stop in then. Trisha will be anxious to see you."

"And I her."

"Please drive carefully."

"Oh, yes. I plan on doing just that, my dear. You girls have a nice day."

"You too, dear."

"It will be one of the best. Bye for now."

As they hung up, Peter couldn't help but realize he had a big grin on his face, and it felt so good. His wife would be so surprised. He had finally figured out what he could get for her that would make her eyes sparkle with love. Now he felt like a young man in his twenties again. All he would need would be for the timing to be just right. Like most things, timing was critical. What he couldn't believe was the fact that he had not thought of it before now. He shook his head at himself as he pulled into the mall.

Now the work would begin. Size, shape, and color were another issue in itself. Sharon was not a person to spend a lot of money, and she wasn't one to flash what she did have. He wanted it to be special and something she would wear always with pride but not in fear of losing it. This would be the last one he would buy for her, and it had to show her just how much he loved her and how he valued her.

Going in and out of stores until he thought there was nothing that would put that sparkle in her eyes that he was wanting to see, he was beginning to feel a weight on his shoulders that he didn't like. This was to be easy and something he would remember as a joyful occasion.

As he walked yet to another store in the mall, he saw it in the window while he was passing by. *Oh my god, that's the one.* It was stunning how the solitaire stood and was lined with smaller diamonds down each side to the halfway point. The band was wide and had three rows of diamonds. The center row of diamonds was larger than the outside row. What a marvel to look at. It was simply stunning. It was the most beautiful set of rings he had ever seen, and it would express his love to Sharon. This would give her the sparkle he was looking for. Now will they have the right size and color?

Finding a clerk was easy as they stood there waiting for their prey. He knew what he wanted although the gentleman tried to sell him others. Peter knew the one in the window was it. It had *Sharon* written all over it. He was able to get it in the silver and the right size. Peter felt he had lucked out, and he knew he would be making his wife very happy. Hell, who was he kidding? It was going to make *him* very happy. It was worth more than she would have ever picked out. Peter didn't care. Sharon was worth it. His life, their future depended on this choice, and he wasn't taking any chances. You know when you see something that just cries out to you and you know it's perfect, the bubbly feeling you get deep down and you want to tell everyone you meet, whether you know them or not.

So Peter made sure he said Merry Christmas to everyone he met. He shook hands with so many people. Some of them looked at him as though he had lost his marbles, but he didn't care. He was going to have the greatest Christmas ever. He hoped he was going to have the best years to come. He and his wife.

ROAD SIDE CROSSES

He realized that Sharon would not want to just move back to the farm and take up living as his wife. Perhaps to him they were still married, but to Sharon, she would have been his common-law wife and that would have never been good enough. Sharon would not have just moved out and started living as a couple, and he couldn't believe how foolish he had been to think that it would have been that simple. He would have destroyed what they all ready had if he had suggested that. God, would he have been making a big mistake? *"Thank you, God, for not letting me make that mistake. Thank you for showing me what the answer was."*

On the way home, he cranked up the radio and sang Christmas songs at the top of his lungs. He didn't think he could be any happier. The only thing was, how was he going to keep it from her? He wasn't good at keeping things from Sharon. She would know he was up to something. He thought, why worry? It was Christmas, and he would just tell her, *"You will have to wait and see."*

He took the ring box out of his pocket, and he flipped it open for one more look. At this point, he couldn't care less if there was anything else under the tree for her. He knew that this was the only important gift that was needed. It would also make Jessy's Christmas perfect. At least he would hope so. How will this make Jessy feel after all these years? Will it make her believe in true love? Will she see that you can make it work if you want it bad enough?

Peter hoped that this would help instill some beliefs for Jessy. He also hoped it would show Sharon that no matter what had happened over the years, he never gave up hope on their dreams. She would have to be his wife to help their dreams come true.

Why had he waited so long? It should have been so simple for him to figure out. With how Sharon had been the last few times, she had been out to the farm and some of the things she would say. Now he felt a little stupid. Sharon had done everything but draw the man a picture, but then you have to know the saying "A picture is worth a thousand words." So perhaps she should have drawn a picture for him and hung it around his neck. What the hell, he got one better, and it goes on her finger. He was sure she would say yes. He was sure this was what Sharon had been wanting for a long time. It was something he had wanted for a long time.

Good God, he knew his wife better than anyone. What took him so long? He could only pray that now the saying "You snooze you lose" doesn't come into play. This would kill him if after all this time Sharon was to say no.

The trip home went fast, and he found everyone at Sharon's. He tucked the ring box into the glove compartment and locked it. His dream was safely locked away until he needed it. He just had to decide when that would be.

Sharon let Trisha answer the door when Peter rang the bell.

"Oh my, you are a sight after a long day." Peter pulled her in for one of his famous bear hugs.

"Hi, Peter," Trisha said as she leaned in to accept the hug he was giving. The love she felt from both Peter and Sharon made coming home worth it.

"Now where is that granddaughter of mine?"

Sharon stepped in for a hug and said, "Sorry, Grandpa. I just put her down. We played her out today with all the shopping."

"Can I go and have a peek, please?"

"Oh yes. The playpen is in the office." Sharon took Peter's hand, and they slipped in quietly. Peter stood and looked at her for a few minutes before he said a word.

"What a precious child. She is so beautiful. She looks like her mom."

"Yes, she does, and what a go-getter she is. Peter, she is so much fun, and she laughs all the time."

"That's good for Trisha."

"Sure is. She has been spoiled with this one. The next one will make up for it."

"What? Is she pregnant again?"

"Oh no, not that I know. I was just saying."

Chapter 26

Christmas Eve had come fast, and with them all out at the farm, it made things easier. There was more room, and they could all spend more time together although it made Peter hide away in his office from time to time.

Shawn had not come but promised that he would make it next year. He took his business seriously, and sometimes, Trisha had said she felt he was married to his job. He was very concerned about providing for her and Crystal in the years to come.

Jessy had seen her dad talking to Mitch earlier, and whatever her dad had said had Mitch smiling and shaking hands with him. With a pat on the back from Peter, Mitch was gone. He was going to see his dad earlier than planned.

Jessy knew he was excited about spending Christmas with his dad, and she was happy for him. She knew she and Mitch would have many more chances to spend Christmas together, but his dad was getting up in age and would have limited Christmases. She hoped this would be the beginning of a new life for Mitch and his father. Perhaps one day they will spend Christmas with Mr. Acorn.

Everyone was sitting around the fire watching Crystal play. She loved all the shiny ornaments on the tree. Sharon had put special ones around the bottom foot of the tree just so Crystal could touch and play with them. After all, what was Christmas all about if not being able to experience the magic of the event? The toddler had brought so much joy this season.

Peter wasn't quite sure how he was going to set this up yet. So he decided to throw it out there and see how well it would be received. "You know what I would like to do this evening? Start a new tradition."

Sharon looked up at him with a surprised look on her face. "Oh? And what might that be, Peter?"

"I would like for all of us to go to Christmas Eve mass tonight."

"Are you turning religious on us, Dad?"

"No, not at all, Jessy. But with Crystal here now, we should take the time and show her that side of Christmas. I was raised with it, and it didn't kill me. When I think about it, it was always a very enjoyable evening."

"Mitch said that's how they always celebrated Christmas Eve. He said they always enjoyed it, especially his mom."

"Well, then, what do you all say? Should we get dressed up in our finest and partake in the festivities at the church?"

"I think it could be fun. What do you say, Mom?"

"Trisha, what do you think? Will Crystal be okay that late?"

"The worst she will do is fall asleep in my arms."

"Okay then, Peter. I think you have a deal. Let's get dressed up."

"If only Mitch would be here."

"Well, if it turns out okay, we can do it again next year and the year after. It might be worth celebrating Christmas Eve in the church."

"Good idea, Dad."

They all went their separate ways to get dressed, and if he knew Sharon, she would have something new and gorgeous to wear for Christmas. She always did. Within the hour, Peter was in his suit, and the girls were in their Christmas dresses and waiting downstairs for Sharon.

"Mom must be getting old."

"Why do you say that, Jessy?"

"It never used to take her so long to get dressed, Trisha, you know that. She used to be ready and calling for us to hurry up."

"So true. I remember."

"It's not like we have to hurry," Peter said to the girls.

"You're right. I'm just excited now, is all. Besides, look at you, Dad. You're pacing the floor like you're nervous."

"It's been a long time since I've been in a church. Maybe they won't let me in." He laughed as he made another pass across the living room. Just then Sharon came downstairs, stopping Peter in his tracks. If he didn't know better, he would have thought Sharon knew what he was up to. She had on a cream-colored pantsuit that had a high collar and beadwork on the shoulders that cascaded down her arms. It was perfect for the occasion. Sharon put her hair up, and that always made her look so elegant. Sharon would always be a knockout no matter how old she got.

"Sharon, you look marvelous."

"You look so sexy in that suit, Peter. I love to see you in it."

"Mom, Dad, you are such a great-looking couple. You make me proud to have you as my parents."

"That makes two of us, Jessy," Trisha said as she went over and wrapped her arm around Jessy's waist.

"Well, now, ladies, should we leave? It could be a little tight for time now." Peter took the long red cape with the hood that was trimmed in off-white fur and helped Sharon put it on. She looked like an angel. It made his heart race with excitement. Everything was going to be great. He just felt like he was on cloud nine.

They got to the church and found the parking lot full, yet there were parking spaces left right outside the door, so he pulled in and parked.

"Peter, do you think we should park here? It must have been left for a reason."

"Sharon, we are already late, so if anyone else is coming, too bad."

"Peter." Sharon slapped him on the arm. He helped all the girls out, and they walked in together as a prayer was being said. They stood at the door entrance until the prayer was over. Sharon noticed Peter looking around nervously, so she took his hand, and as they looked for seats, they found themselves sitting right in the front row.

Peter had looked over his shoulders a couple of times, and Sharon would just squeeze his hand. She couldn't believe how nervous he was. It had been a long time since they had been to church, but good heavens, why would it bother him so much?

The church was decorated to the nines. It was picture-perfect. The house of God was warm and made you feel safe, and it was packed from wall to wall. Everyone was dressed in their finest. Glancing around the room, Peter had seen many of their neighbors. He had not realized so many of them partook in the Christmas Eve mass.

The preacher then gave a nod to Peter, and Peter stood up. Sharon thought he was going to leave, so she reached for his hand to pull him back down.

Peter took hold of her hand, and the room became deadly quiet as Peter said, "Ms. Sharon Sullivan, would you please do me the honor tonight in becoming my wife?"

Sharon put her hand over her mouth as tears come to her eyes.

"Oh, please don't cry, dear." Peter pulled her to her feet, and he could feel her shaking. The whole room was quiet, waiting for her answer.

"So what do you say, sweetheart? Can we get married tonight?"

The tears were flowing as she said, "Oh, Peter." She reached up to touch the side of his face. "I thought you would never ask."

A loud cheer went up, and the clapping began as Peter took her into a bear hug and whispered, "Thank you." He looked down at the girls, and both Jessy and Trisha were crying and holding on to each other.

The preacher then interrupted and asked them to go to the front. The woman who had been playing the piano walked over and gave Sharon a hug along with a bouquet of Christmas holly and small white flowers. It was just so beautiful and perfect. He then asked them who would be their witnesses, and Sharon turned to Jessy, reaching out her hand as Peter looked back at the door and had Jessy's eyes following him. They saw Mitch coming through with his arm intertwined in the arm of his father as they made their way up to the front row, with Mr. Acorn taking a seat beside Trisha.

Jessy gasped and put her hand up over her mouth. Mitch handed her the band that would be placed onto her father's finger, and the tears began to flow. Mitch pulled her in for a hug and whispered, "Everything is okay, Jess."

Peter just stood with a wide grin. Trisha could only sit and cry as she rocked her baby. This would be a Christmas to remember and one she would talk to Crystal about for many years to come. The only way it would have been more perfect for them was if Shawn would have been there. Trisha had to tune herself back into what the preacher was saying.

"Peter has written his own vow to Sharon that he would like to share at this time."

"Sharon, I want to wake up beside you for the rest of my life. I want us to grow old together the way we were meant to, holding hands and making memories to chase away the rain clouds. I love the way you fit into my arms and the tender way you look at me. You are my vision at the end of a busy day. You are my moon, my stars, and my life. You are and always will be my love. I love you, Sharon."

The tears were falling from Sharon, not for sadness but for the joy she was feeling from the only man she had ever loved.

The preacher then said, "Sharon, do you have a reply for Peter? We know it is short notice and you didn't come prepared to be married tonight." This brought a chuckle from the crowd.

Sharon takes a moment to get herself in check, and as she looked up to the love of her life, she spoke from the heart. "Of all the people in the world and all the ones I have met in my lifetime, it was a miracle I ever found you. I wasn't looking for love. It just happened. You were so kind and considerate. I loved seeing you, talking with you, and spending time with you. I couldn't picture my life without you. Although we have been living apart, my love for you never died. So thank you for making my dream come true tonight and wanting to finish our lives together as God had intend so many years ago. I love you, Peter, and I always will."

There were sounds of gasps, awws, and sniffles coming from the crowd.

When it came time for them to exchange rings, it was Sharon who gasped, and the tears were flowing. "Oh, Peter, they're perfect."

"No, you're perfect, and you were meant for me. I love you, Sharon."

"And I love you, Peter."

"You may kiss your bride."

As Peter took his wife into his arms and kissed her with such tenderness, another cheer went up and the festivities started. It was a different Christmas Eve celebrated tonight in the church and one they would talk about for many years.

"Mom, Dad, you have just given me the perfect Christmas. As long as I should live, there will never be anything that will ever come close. Thank you. I love you both so very much." Jessy snuggled in close to her parents, and they wrapped their arms around her.

"We are glad to have made you happy, Jessy, but remember, you're young and have many Christmases ahead of you and many more surprises."

"Speaking of surprises," Jessy said as she left to go over to Mitch's side. "Hey, Mitch."

"Hi, Jess. I would like you to meet my dad, Ed Acorn."

"Mr. Acorn, I'm so pleased to meet you. Merry Christmas."

"That it is, dear, that it is. I have heard so much about you. I feel like I have known you for a long time."

Jessy felt her face flush as she answered him, "I have heard lots about you as well, sir."

"Seems like my son likes to talk." He put his hand upon Mitch's shoulder. Jessy couldn't help but notice how much Mitch looked like his father.

"Mr. Acorn, are you and Mitch going to join us for Christmas dinner tomorrow?"

"Mitch told me you do a Christmas dinner for the homeless. I would like to help."

Smiling, she said, "That would be so kind of you. We would love to have your help."

"Then that is settled. We will have dinner together."

As the evening wound done and all the people started to leave, Peter went to find Sharon. "My darling, are you ready to go home now?"

"Home, Peter?"

"Yes, dear. Sorry, but tomorrow is Christmas, and our daughter would not like it if we weren't under the same roof as she."

Sharon snuggled in close. "Peter, I'm coming home after all these years."

"I really don't know what took me so long, Sharon. I'm sorry."

"Don't be sorry. We are one again, and that's all that counts. I love you."

"I love you too."

"Peter, how did you come to this conclusion anyways? How did you manage to do all this? You have totally surprised me, that is for sure."

"A good surprise, I hope."

"The best, but you still didn't answer me."

"Well, my dear, I asked for help in finding a way of bringing you home. This was the answer that was presented to me. The Lord works in mysterious ways. Now let's get the gang and go home."

Peter was never any happier than he was right now. His family was whole again, and it was all because he had faith in both himself and God. He said a silent prayer as they were about to leave the church.

"Thank you. I am forever in your debt."

Chapter 27

The night was a dream come true for Sharon, Peter, and Jessy. Jessy felt like she had waited her whole life to be a whole family. Although after so long it felt normal the way they were, she just felt there was something missing: the unity that made a family whole. She was so happy on the inside, and all she could do was smile, hugging her mom and dad every chance she got. She had pinched herself at one point just to make sure it wasn't a dream.

It was something that had been her dream for so long. Jessy had prayed many nights for her parents to find a way back to each other as one. She had always thought that her mom would just move back in. She never dreamed of them ever remarrying, but her dad had found the perfect answer, and she should have known if anyone could find the answer, her dad would. Why it took so long, she had no idea and wanted to ask him. Right now, she would just wallow in her happiness. She didn't think she would even be able to sleep, afraid of waking up and finding it was just a dream after all.

Their house was full of Christmas cheer. Mitch and his dad had gone out to the farm for a couple of drinks then they left to go to Mitch's with the promise of returning tomorrow. Jessy was happy for Mitch, to see him with his dad. She of all people knew just how he was feeling tonight, and she hoped for their sake it would last.

Tomorrow would be another great day. They all would be working at the town hall giving Christmas to the homeless. On their way home from the church, she had noticed the town tree was full of gifts for the homeless. Whenever Jessy saw that kind of response from people, it made her cry. She found it overwhelming.

Once Crystal was put to bed, they sat around and enjoyed the rest of the evening in peace. With Christmas carols playing softly in the background, Jessy watched the love between her mom and dad glow. She felt that if there was nothing else under the tree, it wouldn't matter. God had already given her the one thing she had asked for. Her Santa had really outdone himself this year. This would be a hard act to follow. There would never be another Christmas like it. Especially Christmas Eve.

Christmas morning was a noisy one, with Crystal opening her gifts. She had so many that she had to be put down for a nap before they left for the hall. It didn't matter if it took her all day to open gifts. There was no rush. Trisha wasn't leaving until the 28, so Crystal had plenty of time.

Sharon and Peter had an aura around them that shone like a bright light. It was true that there was only one true love per person on this earth, and they differently were a match made in heaven. Jessy had never seen so much love. It was like they had kept it all bottled up inside, and now that they were one, it was released. She always knew her mom and dad loved each other, but what she didn't realize was that it was to such an extreme. She hoped that one day she will have that love. Now that she had seen the difference between love and real love, Jessy felt it was going to be hard to find.

The day at the town hall went by fast, and everyone ate their fill of Christmas dinner. Sharon had her dinner cooking at home and would do the final touches when they got home.

Mr. Acorn had fit right in, and he chatted up with many of the homeless. He seemed to love helping out. He and Mitch had shared a few laughs throughout, the day and it warmed Jessy's heart. She knew Mitch was having the best Christmas ever. This year, she and Mitch had a lot in common when it came to Christmas. She knew that when Christmas was all over and everyone went back to their normal lives, they would sit and talk of this Christmas for many hours to come. She was looking forward to hearing all about his dad. She was also interested in knowing all the details of her mom and dad's wedding. After all, Mitch had a big role to play in it, and it pleased her to see that her dad had included Mitch in their special event. This told her that her dad cared a lot about Mitch. She had always known that her parents liked Mitch, but for her dad to have consulted with Mitch and not her spoke volumes.

Poor Crystal was getting worn out, and it looked like Trisha was getting anxious to go home. She said she missed Shawn; she had had a great time, but now she was missing him. She thought that perhaps that was what was wrong with Crystal. Her daddy played with her every chance he had, and Crystal adored her father.

So as December 28 came, Jessy and Mitch had gone back to work and Trisha was heading home. Trisha was happy, yet deep down inside she knew she would miss the only family that had ever shown her what love was all about. Her life was now to be with Shawn, and she hoped that they too could have what Sharon and Peter have. Trisha also hoped it wouldn't take that many years.

Crystal was packed in the back of the SUV with what new toys they were taking home all within her reach. Trisha had her in the middle of the backseat and all her things packed in around her. She said once she got driving, Crystal would sleep, so if they didn't have to stop, Crystal would sleep all the way home.

There had been a new snowfall overnight, and Trisha was giving herself plenty of time. With an all-wheel drive, she felt safe on the roads.

"Trisha, please call us when you get home. We want to know you and Crystal are home safe."

"I will, Peter."

He pulled her in for one of his bear hugs. Trisha loved him with all her heart. He was her father no matter what, and he made her feel so safe and loved. Crystal would know what a loving grandfather he was as she got older.

"Thank you, Sharon, for everything. I had the best Christmas ever."

Taking Trisha into her arms as a mother would do, Sharon whispered in her ear, "Remember, dear, I love you and you, and Crystal are always welcome here anytime." They embraced for a short moment longer, Trisha not wanting to let go. This was her safe haven, and she loved them with all her heart.

She had thought of her real parents while she was there, but there was no way she could bring herself to call them. Mitch had brought it up for a short time, but Trisha didn't know him well enough to really get into details. She figured Jessy probably had told him about her life, but she doesn't want to go down that road right now. Perhaps another day, she told him. He respected that and changed the subject.

Trisha waved to them all as she drove away with a smile on her face but an ache in her heart.

Sharon and Peter went back into their quiet, empty house.

"You know, Sharon, we are all alone."

"Yes, we are. It's so good to have them all home but equally good to see them all leave. Do you think that is being selfish, Peter?" She went in and sat down on the love seat.

"Not at all. You took care of everyone, and now you need a break. Nothing selfish about that. I will get us coffee." Peter went in and sat down beside her, putting their coffee on the end table.

"Thank you." She put her head on his shoulder. They sat there in silence for a bit, not sharing any thoughts then Sharon said, "You know, Peter, I am exhausted. I must be getting old."

"Me too. It has been a very busy week. You know, we could go upstairs. We are alone and will be for a few days. Why don't we have our own honeymoon right here? Neither one of us have to report to work. My hands are taking care of things for a few more days, so I don't have to go outside if I don't want to."

"That sounds like a great idea. I would love it, but I have to warn you, I feel like I could sleep for a week."

"I'm sure I can keep you awake for a little longer." Peter took her hand, and they disappeared without any worries or concerns of the outside world. For whatever time they could steal, it would only be them and the love they shared.

Peter and Sharon drifted off to sleep shortly after their lovemaking. It amazed them at how great it still was between them. They both hoped that their sex life would stay strong through their later years. Having talked about the what-ifs and the possibility of poor health, they had agreed that no matter what was to come, they would see it through because of their love, not basing their marriage on sex and just knowing that they were truly loved would be enough.

Chapter 28

Jessy and Mitch were finding things to do around the station. It looked like it was going to be a quiet day, which they didn't mind, seeing how they were just getting back from Christmas break and looking forward to the New Year. There wasn't usually too much happening at 4 a.m., but as people wake up, so do the phones.

Mitch was happy that he and his dad would be spending more time together. They had a great time at Christmas, and Mitch had promised his dad that he would be over to see him more often. Mr. Acorn was pleased to know that his son hadn't held any resentment for the way he had been over the years. Mitch just seemed to be happy to know that they now could move on without his mom after all this time. His dad was a man with a big heart, and Mitch knew that when his mom died, it took a big part of his dad. He knew his dad loved him and was in extreme pain from his loss. He felt giving him time to heal was the only thing he could do.

Mitch was glad that the healing was finally done, and he and his father could move on having a life together. So to him, the New Year was full of promises and dreams.

He knew they had plenty of making up to do. So his fishing days would be plentiful and anything else his dad wanted to do. Perhaps they could travel and see some of the places he had heard his dad say he would like to see. These thoughts had Mitch's mind full, and it made him quiet around the station as he was deep in thought.

Jessy was deep with her own thoughts. The fact that her mom and dad had remarried and made their family complete couldn't have pleased her more. It was something she had prayed for but never thought would actually happen. She had always known they still loved one another, but they both were two very strong-minded people. Why her dad had waited so long to make things whole again was something she would never understand. Perhaps the timing was right. She knew about timing and how everything happens for a reason, whether we agree with it or not. The universe has a strange way of running things; we are just along for the ride.

This Christmas would be one that she would never forget, and it would make for a great love story to tell her children someday.

Watching Trisha with Crystal had opened Jessy's eyes to the fact that there was more to life than working all the time. Jessy felt that when the time came for her to become a wife and a mother, she would be ready for it. In an odd kind of way, she envied Trisha for what she had. To know that there was someone at home who loved you unconditionally had to be the greatest feeling of all.

"Hey, Jess, it's time to take a break. Let's run to Timmy's."

"It's about time. I'm almost worn out already."

Dropping what they were doing, they left for Timmy's.

"We have put in a long day, and we just got started."

"It feels like we have been here for a long time."

Being deep in thought dragged out the morning, and as Jessy looked at her watch, she said to Mitch, "Trisha should be on the road by now, unless Mom and Dad detained her for another day."

"I don't think your mom will be happy to see them leave."

"No. She will miss them, especially Crystal. Mom likes being a grandmother."

"Your folks sure seem to be happy."

"Yeah, I think they are very happy."

"You too, Jess."

"That I am. I didn't think it would ever happen."

"It was a pleasant surprise when your dad asked me to stand up for him. I was very honored to be asked."

"Yeah, you sneak, and you never said a word."

"It was part of his Christmas present to you and your mom. How could I say anything?"

"Thank you for being there for Dad. I know it meant a lot to him, having you do that."

"It was my pleasure. It was fun to watch it all go down. Especially the look on you and your mom's face."

"I felt like I was in a dream. It was such a strange feeling, probably because I hadn't expected it. Everything was so out of the ordinary for us, with us going to midnight mass and all. Dad has pulled some surprises over the years, but that had topped them all."

"Well, Jess, it seemed to have made a big difference in you."

"I'm totally happy now. My heart is at ease, and it's a good feeling. I think I was always worried that either Mom or Dad would find another partner, and I didn't want that because I knew they still loved each other. I'm so glad that Dad finally woke up and put an end to all my worries."

"I'm happy for you, Jess, that it all has worked itself out."

"I'm happy for you, Mitch. To have your dad back in your life, you must feel as I do, relieved."

"I was worried going over to see him and asking about coming for Christmas. When I got there, he was helping some homeless man and woman, and he was so happy that I took the gamble of asking him right then, and he was grateful I had gone back. He said he was going to ask me when he had seen us, but he thought perhaps I hadn't forgiven him. So he decided not to say a word."

"It's funny how things change so quickly, yet it took so long for both my parents and your dad to see what had to be changed. But I, for one, am very thankful that it has all turned out well."

"That makes two of us, Jess. I'm looking forward to the New Year with my dad."

"Me as well, with my parents as one."

Their radio went off, which jolted them back to the present. The wreck was at the big bridge out of town. They heard all the calls going back and forth and how the fire rescue trucks had been dispatched. The way the talk was, it was serious and more than one vehicle was involved. Jessy and Mitch were in a long line of emergency vehicles. With police lights coming from all directions, it caused a chill to run across Jessy's body.

"Good Lord. This can't be good, Mitch."

"I would say not."

"What a way to end your Christmas holiday."

"Or start. Perhaps someone was just leaving on theirs."

"Either way, it sucks."

As they got closer, they could see people everywhere at the entrance of the bridge.

"What the hell, Jess."

"Oh, good Lord, Mitch, looks like someone has gone over the side."

They were waved in to the far end and were told someone was being pulled out of the water. Mitch had turned their unit around and backed in as close as he could get. It was snowing, and the wind chill was biting. Mitch and Jessy had the stretcher out and were running for the bank. They could see it was a child, a very small child.

As the fire rescue member placed the child down on the stretcher, Jessy's head began to spin as Mitch said, "Oh my god, Jessy."

"Oh, God. It can't be, Mitch, it's Crystal. Where's the baby's mother?"

"She is still in her vehicle. She is trapped under the steering wheel," the rescue worker said as he stood back.

As Mitch checked for a heartbeat, Jessy was trying to wrap what parts of Crystal were exposed to the weather.

"She has no heartbeat, Jess. You take her to the unit and get her inside quickly. We will bring up the stretcher. Now go. It will be faster than strapping her down right now."

The two men took the stretcher as Jessy took Crystal, and they raced up to their unit, getting Crystal inside.

Mitch said, "God, Jess, she isn't doing well."

Jessy could hear the panic in Mitch's voice. Trying to give mouth to mouth on one so small was difficult. Performing CPR was also somewhat difficult.

"Come on, little one," was all Mitch could say as he worked on Crystal. They had lost track of the time, and to Jessy, it seemed like it was impossible.

"It's no use, Mitch, we have lost her." Tears welled up in Jessy's eyes as she put her hand over her mouth.

"No, damn it." Mitch wasn't giving up. He was giving it one more shot. Jessy was starting to feel very weak at the knees when they heard a faint cry.

"Mitch, did you hear that? She cried."

"Come on, little girl, you can do this." Mitch flipped Crystal to her side, and she started to cough out water and cry all at the same time.

"Thank God." Jessy stripped Crystal of all her wet clothes and, taking a towel, used it as a diaper of sorts and then wrapped her up in a warm blanket while Mitch got an IV running. Crystal was blue as she was cold.

"Oh, Mitch, she is so cold, the poor little thing."

"Remember to warm her up slowly, Jessy, and I will go see what's going on with Trisha before we take Crystal in." He saw the tears in Jessy's eyes and knew she was on the verge of a breakdown.

"Come on, Jess. Stay with me on this. Crystal needs you, okay? You going to be okay while I go see about Trisha?"

Jessy just nodded as she picked Crystal up to put her against her body to warm her up.

Mitch ran down the bank to see what was happening. There were more people now than before. There were divers on the bank, and they were taking turns. Mitch had found out there were two vehicles in the water, a car and Trisha's SUV. He was told that a big truck had gone sideways on the ice first and wiped out the guardrail. The other vehicles hit the ice and had nothing to stop them from going over.

Trisha was stuck inside as the SUV had sunk even further. The hatch on the back had popped open, which had given them access to Crystal and to Trisha. Getting Crystal out of her chair was easy, but Trisha was stuck under the steering wheel, and the front end had sunk deep into the water. It wasn't deep enough to drown her, but the cold water was going to be hard on her. Trisha was unconscious, and they doubted very much that she would make it. Between the head trauma and the cold water, she wasn't going to have much of a chance.

The couple in the car was in just as bad a shape although they were out and on their way to the hospital. Mitch was sick. How was he going to tell Jessy about Trisha and her chances? There was nothing he could do, so he and Jessy would take Crystal to the hospital. Running back up to his unit, he felt so weak at the knees. It was a good thing he didn't have far to run.

When he told Jessy what had happened and what they thought Trisha's chances were, Jessy sat with Crystal in her arms and rocked while she cried.

"Jessy, we're not staying. We're taking Crystal in now. She needs more care. So hang in there, okay, sweetheart?" He kissed her on top of her head and put a hand on Crystal's face, thinking to himself *Jessy was right. Crystal was so damn cold.*

Mitch had managed to call Peter and Sharon once they had Crystal in the hospital. Jessy wasn't leaving Crystal's side. She was still in danger, and she had no mommy at her side. This tore at Jessy's heart. What would happen to Crystal now? Would Shawn keep her, or would Trisha's parents get her?

They brought Trisha in about twenty minutes after Mitch and Jessy had gotten to the hospital. Jessy met them at the door, taking Trisha's hand as they wheeled her through to emergency. Trisha was also cold, and she had blood everywhere from the head trauma that she had received, and her color was horrible. Jessy figured Trisha was already dead.

Peter and Sharon found Jessy sobbing into her hands in the waiting room. Crystal had been taken down for x-rays.

"Jessy, where is Trisha?" Peter asked.

"She is in there, Dad. She's not in good shape." Jessy had pointed to the double doors of the emergency room. Jessy broke down as did Sharon.

"What happened, Mitch?" Peter had Sharon wrapped in his arms now. Mitch had sat down to wrap his arms around Jessy. She was now shaking like a leaf. Mitch went on to tell them what he had been told had happened.

"What do you think Trisha's chances are?"

"I would have to say, Peter, slim to none."

"Oh my god. Jessy, do you have Shawn's number? He will be waiting for them. I will call him."

"Yes, I do, Dad." She dug through her purse and found her cell phone. At first, she couldn't remember his last name. Her mind had gone blank. "I can't think straight."

"Calm down, Jess, and take a couple of deep breaths. It will come to you," Mitch said as he rubbed her back.

Peter had called Shawn and told him what had happened. Shawn was having a pilot friend fly him out. The chopper could land right at the hospital. Peter was to let the hospital know he was on his way.

A beautiful Christmas and a good morning turned tragic in a blink of an eye.

Chapter 29

When Crystal was brought back, they had been told she had a fractured left leg along with all her bruising. She was moved into the nursery, where they would keep a close watch on her. They wanted to bring her body temperature up slowly. Then in a couple of days, if all was well, they would let her go. They were worried about her catching pneumonia. It was very likely to happen after all Crystal had been through.

Shawn had arrived before they had heard anything on Trisha's condition. Her outcome was not good. Trisha was considered brain dead and was on life support. Now there were serious decisions to be made. When Shawn was told of her condition, he just dropped to his knees and cried.

Peter squatted down beside him and pulled him into his embrace. "I'm here, son." Tears were flowing down Peter's face as much as they were on Shawn's. After a couple of minutes, Peter stood up, and he pulled Shawn to his feet and took him over to a chair. The man was so broken it had Peter worried. How can any man in this condition make decisions such as the ones they were wanting with Trisha?

"Would you like coffee, Shawn?"

"No thanks. I want to see Trisha and my daughter."

"I will see if you can go in yet." Peter went to the nurse's station and asked. There was no problem. The nurse was taking Shawn in to see his family.

"Shawn, are you going to be okay alone, seeing Trisha?"

Shawn just nodded.

"Sharon and I have to leave for a short time, but we will be back as soon as we can, all right?"

Again Shawn just nodded. Peter patted him on the back as he turned to walk away.

At this time, Peter and Sharon decided to go and see Mike and Pearl. It wasn't something they would want to hear over the phone if it were their daughter, so they felt it was only right they went to tell them in person.

Peter and Sharon cried all the way there.

"We have to get ourselves together before we go to their door, Sharon," Peter said.

Blowing her nose and wiping her face seemed endless. Sharon didn't think the tears would ever stop. "Why, Peter? She has a baby to take care of."

"They are called horrible accidents for that reason, dear."

As they pulled up into the drive, all Peter could say was, "We should have made her come see them while she was here. It will be hard for them to know she was this close for Christmas with their grandchild and they didn't get to say good-bye."

"Oh, Peter, I know, but who was to know this would happen?"

"Sharon, we know you can't know what lies ahead, so we should have made her come. I'm sure we could have talked her into it. Trisha might have been upset with us, but she would have done it all the same because we asked her to. Mike and Pearl will never forgive us, Sharon. I won't blame them."

Sharon reached over and took his hand. "Let's take it one day at a time, okay?"

The surprised look on Mike's and Pearl's faces to see Peter and Sharon at their door was nothing compared to the look once Peter told them why they were there.

How Sharon found the strength she needed to handle Pearl was more than she knew. At that point, she was like Jessy, and she just stepped right in and handled whatever it was she needed at that very moment. Sharon knew she would have plenty of time to mourn once she and Peter were back home.

Mike and Pearl took it very hard. Sharon was surprised that they had asked for coffee instead of going for the bottle.

Pearl turned to Peter and asked, "Would you be kind enough to take us to the hospital to see our daughter and granddaughter? I know I can't drive, and I don't think Mike should either."

"I wouldn't mind at all."

"Let us change our clothes. We will be just a few minutes. Come, Mike, let's get ready and go see our daughter." Pearl took him by the hand and helped him out of his chair.

Mike was a big man, yet he looked like he had just shrunk right into a shell. All the time Peter was telling them what they knew, Mike said nothing. There wasn't even a tear. Peter figured he was in shock and would fall apart after he had seen for his own eyes the shape his daughter was in.

Their trip back to the hospital was in silence. Tears rolled down Pearl's cheeks as with Sharon's. Both Peter and Sharon were right. Mike and Pearl loved their daughter; there was no doubt about it. They just weren't parents.

Peter and Sharon found Jessy and Mitch with Shawn. They were all sitting around Trisha's bed.

Pearl stumbled looking for a chair when she saw her daughter and sat crying uncontrollably. Sharon tried to console her, but Pearl wasn't hearing a thing.

Mike went over to his daughter, and taking her by the hand, he lowered his head and kissed her. He whispered, "Hey, peanut, Daddy's here now. You will be safe." He stayed with her for about five minutes before he stood up straight, and putting his hand upon his chest, he said, "God, if you are taking my little girl, please don't let her suffer. That's all I will ask of you."

He then kissed his daughter again. "Remember, peanut, I will always love you." Then with a quick glance at his wife, he left the room.

"Pearl, would you like to talk to Trisha?" Sharon asked her.

Blowing her nose, Pearl nodded. Sharon took Pearl by the arm and helped her to the side of the bed.

Shawn was still standing on the other side of the bed, holding on to Trisha's hand. The tears were slowly flowing, and Peter's heart ached for him. He couldn't imagine being in Shawn's boots right now. He could only be thankful that it wasn't Sharon or Jessy lying there. Knowing it was Trisha and she had been like a daughter to them hurt like hell, but he knew he had to hold it together for his family and for Shawn. He would have plenty of time to release his anger when he went to the barn. For now, he would be the pillar that they all needed.

Sharon had taken the chair that Pearl had vacated, and Pearl wasn't holding any tears back. She kept telling Trisha over and over that she would be okay and that they would take her home and take care of her.

Shawn finally snapped, and he got everyone's attention. Peter went over and put a hand on his shoulder. "No, she won't be okay, and no, you're taking her home now or ever. Do you understand? She is gone already. It's a matter of saying good-bye."

"What are you talking about? I'm not saying good-bye to my daughter. Not yet. She is too young and has a baby to raise."

"Pearl, this is as good as it's going to get for Trisha. Your daughter is brain dead. That machine there is breathing for her to keep her organs alive until some decisions are made, then the plug will be pulled. So no, she isn't coming home." His voice got quiet as he continued to say, "Not in body, anyway. I'm sorry."

Pearl got very agitated, and Sharon had gone and gotten a nurse. Pearl was given a sedative to calm her down. The nurse said she would sleep and it would be best if she was taken home. Peter said he would take her. Mitch and Jessy were going back to check on the baby. Sharon was staying with Shawn. When everyone left, it gave Sharon time to talk to Shawn.

"Shawn, are you okay?"

"No, madam, I'm not."

"I can't begin to tell you how sorry we are that this happened to Trisha and to you."

Shawn didn't say much then he said, "What am I supposed to do now?"

"Well, you go on the best you can, Shawn. It's going to be tough at first. Time will heal, and things will get easier."

"How do I let those people keep her lying here like this until they are ready to accept that she is gone? It's not right. I can't keep coming back and forth. Trisha doesn't even know I'm here. God, she is already dead." He wept again.

"You know, Shawn, the choice will be yours."

"What do you mean?"

"Weren't you and Trisha living together?"

Looking a little sheepish, he said, "Yes, madam. We have been for some time now. Why?"

"I think that gives you the power to decide when that machine is stopped. You would be considered her spouse now."

"Do you really think so?"

"Yes, I do."

"Oh, God. I don't think I could make that call. What if . . ." He said no more. "What if the doctors are wrong?"

"Yeah, mistakes have been made before."

"Yes, they have, but they would do tests again to make sure there is no brain activity before they would let you decide to end it."

"How can I take Crystal's mom away forever?"

"Like you said, Shawn, to Pearl, she is already gone. That machine is breathing for her until decisions are made."

"I didn't know I would be making them."

"Do you know if Trisha ever had a will made up?"

"Oh yes, madam, as soon as she had Crystal. She felt that it was very important."

"Then maybe you won't be having to make the decision."

"What do you mean?"

"Why don't you get her will and see if she had anything put in it for this situation?"

"I don't want to leave her now."

"Shawn, she is not going anywhere, and they will be wanting to know if she wanted to donate any organs. Please you go home and get it. I will stay with Trisha until you come back."

"But what if someone . . ." He couldn't finish his sentence.

"Shawn, no one is going to pull that plug until you are back and her will is read, I promise."

"Okay. I will be back tomorrow. I will check in on Crystal before I leave." Shawn kissed Trisha, and a heavy sob caught in his throat. Sharon went around to his side, and he cried on her shoulder as she held him.

His crying had gotten Sharon to crying. She hadn't wanted that to happen. This boy needed her strength, not her weakness. When Shawn had gotten himself together and left Sharon found, she needed Peter badly.

Sharon was holding Trisha's hand, and the tears were slipping from her eyes no matter how hard she tried to control them.

"Mom, are you all right?"

"Oh, Jessy. Why did this have to happen? She is so young."

"I have asked the same question, Mom, many times in the last few hours."

"It's so hard sitting here knowing she is already gone, yet it looks like she is just sleeping and could wake up any moment, I just want to scream." Jessy hugged her mother. She knew Sharon loved Trisha as much as she loved her.

When Peter came back, Jessy had excused herself. She was going to the bathroom to cry. In there she could cry as hard as she wanted to. She had lost her best friend, the closest person she had to a sister. Now they would lose contact with Shawn and Crystal as they made their new life together. There was no reason for Shawn to ever come back once Trisha was laid to rest. So today they didn't just lose Trisha—they lost Crystal as well.

Then Jessy thought, *Oh my god.* What was going to happen to her mom when she realizes what she had just realized?

Jessy was feeling totally empty inside, and lost. She would spend as much time with Crystal as she could while she was in the hospital. It was probably going to be the last time they would see her. Mitch had left and gone to the station to file their reports. He was going to do Jessy's for her and explain to everyone why she would be away for a while.

He knew Jessy was taking it very hard and the fact that she was also worried about the baby and what would become of her. No one knew Shawn very well, so not knowing what kind of life he was going to provide for their daughter had Jessy worried, and at this point, it was anyone's guess.

When Jessy saw Shawn in with Crystal, he seemed to be a loving father, and Crystal responded to his love. Jessy could see the bond that was between them. It pleased her to know that just maybe they would be enough to see each other through the hard days to come. Mitch hoped that seeing this was going to help Jessy deal with the loss of her friend and not have to worry about the baby.

Peter, Sharon, and Jessy slept in shifts, or at least tried to get some rest at the hospital. They rotated turns with Trisha and Crystal, not wanting to leave either of them alone. They knew deep down they were wishing for a miracle and were waiting for Trisha to wake up.

Chapter 30

In the morning, they all took turns going home showering and changing. Mitch had come back for a short time just to check on them all. He was still on duty. He was working with the replacement that Jessy had worked with while he was off. Jessy knew he was in good hands with Emily Becon. She knew her work and didn't miss a beat. This made Jessy relax about work and not have to worry about the extra load she had just put on Mitch. He and Emily would make a good team while she was off.

Shawn had called and said he would be back around two. He had to see their lawyer before he left.

When Sharon went back to the hospital, she had brought with her a small stereo. She wanted to play soft music for Trisha. She didn't care if they told her she no longer could hear them. She wasn't willing to let Trisha go yet. After all, God does work in mysterious ways.

Jessy was concerned about her mom, and she knew that Sharon wouldn't accept Trisha's fate easily. Trisha was Sharon's daughter in all the ways that mattered. Jessy knew that she and Peter were going to have hard days ahead as well, not only with the mourning of Trisha and losing Crystal but also with a distraught mother and wife. They could only pray for the strength that they would all need.

Shawn was right on time. He had gone in and kissed Trisha and checked on everyone before going down to see Crystal, picking her up and sitting in the rocking chair with her while he talked to her. Crystal snuggled right into his chest as she always had done.

"Daddy loves you, little girl, and you know that Mommy loves you too. We will miss Mommy always, but we will have her in our memories and, most of all, in our hearts. I want you to know that whatever I do from here on is what I think is best for you. I can only hope that as you get older, you will understand and that you will forgive me. There will never be a day that I won't think of you and your mommy. I want you to always remember that you are Daddy's little girl, and I will always love you. I'm sorry I don't have any other choice."

Shawn held Crystal tight as the tears rolled down his face. He sat and rocked and cried with Crystal until she had her afternoon snack. He knew his daughter needed to be put down to get a good sleep. Crystal loved to be rocked, but she liked to be in her bed to sleep. Kissing his daughter and tucking her in tore at his heart like no man should ever have to feel. This just wasn't right. Shawn was a big believer in the saying "Things happen for a reason." Just what the hell the reason for this was, he would never understand. Why take a mother from her baby who would need her more?

Shawn knew that Peter, Sharon, and Jessy were all waiting for him. He had hoped that Mitch would also be there. He felt that Jessy would need someone to hold her. Although her parents would be there, he knew that it should be Mitch. Trisha would have wanted him at her side at a time like this, so he was going to put the meeting off as long as he could. Mitch had to be there.

As it was by the time Shawn had gone back to Trisha's room, Mitch had shown up. He was on the early shift.

Going into Trisha's room was the most agonizing thing he had to do. He knew she was already dead; it was just a matter of all the paperwork. Everyone except Jessy was sitting. Jessy had a hold of Trisha's hand and was stroking her hair, talking to her in a soft voice, talking about their lives together as teens.

Shawn just stood inside the door and listened. He could tell by what Jessy was saying that the girls had shared as much in their younger years as any sisters would have. It was no wonder this family was so close to Trisha and Trisha to them. Shawn had always known how much Trisha had loved this family, and in some ways, he never understood. They weren't blood related, but no one would have known.

It just blew him away to find out that they had all stayed at the hospital all night long to be with his daughter and the woman who was to become his wife that summer. That thought ripped through his heart.

His wife, the sleeping beauty who lay waiting to be awakened by a magical kiss. It pained him to know he didn't have that magical power. It was something that only happened in fairy tales.

Peter had turned and saw Shawn standing in the door. Going over to him, he shook his hand and said, "Hi, son. How are you holding up?"

Shawn just nodded as he knew he would break down so easily in front of this loving family.

"I'm going to get us all coffees. Would you like one? I'm making a run to Timmy's."

That brought a slight smile to Shawn's face as he said, "I would love one. Thanks."

Jessy kissed Trisha and backed away for Shawn to be able to get closer to her. Shawn so wanted to see that she had moved or something different, but it was all exactly the same as it was when he had left yesterday.

Sharon, Jessy, and Mitch all left the room, giving Shawn his time with Trisha. They went down to wait for Peter in the waiting room.

"This has to be tearing that young man up inside. I don't know what he has for family. Why is no one here for him?"

"Maybe someone will be coming, Mom. Give it time. It's not like Trisha is going anywhere."

"I know that, but he needs someone now."

"Guess we will just have to make sure we are here for him in whichever way he needs us."

"That's nice of you, Mitch, but he seems like a real loner. When Jessy and I went to see Trisha, we never even met him. He never came around. Trisha said he stays at work very long hours."

"He's a workaholic. Could be worse."

"Yes, Mitch, it could be, but now he has a little girl to take care of. He won't be able to work like that."

"I guess he will have to figure it out. Surely he has family there to help."

"That's something we never asked about. We thought there was lots of time. Besides, they were getting married this summer. We would have met them all then."

"Oh, Mom, I forgot about that." Jessy put her hand over her mouth as tears came again so easily.

"Here we go, people. Coffee and doughnuts. Not much of a meal, but we can all get by on a sugar high for a while."

"Thanks, dear."

"Thanks, Dad."

"Yes, thank you, Peter."

"You're all welcome. Should we take Shawn his so he can join us?"

"I think that's a great idea, dear."

When they got back to the room, they found Shawn sitting in a chair with papers opened up in his hand and crying.

Sharon went over and put her hand on his shoulder. "Son, Peter has brought your coffee."

He looked up, and at that moment, Sharon saw the look of a broken man. He had the look of a young boy who so badly needed his mom. Was that something he and Trisha had in common, lack of parenting while growing up? Is that what brought them together?

Sharon's heart ached for this young man who sat here in grief all alone. Or at least in his world, he must feel all alone.

Shawn took the coffee and drank it slowly before he said, "I have Trisha's will. I would like to read it to you."

"To us? Are you sure, Shawn?"

"Yes, I want all of you to hear this."

Mitch stood up and excused himself. "I will wait outside."

"No, I want you to hear this as well."

Mitch stopped short as he hesitated.

"Please. I think you should be included in the reading. I want you to be. It's important to me."

Mitch looked around at the others, and no one said a word. Jessy walked over and slipped her hand into his. "Please, Mitch, for Trisha."

Mitch wasn't comfortable with this. He hardly knew these people. Why would he have to hear what Trisha had written in her will? Looking at Jessy, he knew he should stay for her. Reading of a will is a sure sign that someone had passed away. It makes it final.

"All right, I will stay."

"Thank you," Shawn said as he opened up the papers again that he was holding and began to read with shaking hands.

The first part was all the same as it was in everyone's will, but as he got deeper into the will, it became harder for him to read. The part about if she were ever to be pronounced brain dead, her good organs were to be harvested for anyone who needed them. Shawn had a real hard time with this. Although it was her wish, he couldn't imagine someone else with her body parts. Trisha was very adamant that she wanted to help whoever she could. She believed in what came around, went around. She would not be around to help someone as Peter, Sharon, and Jessy had done for her, so in return, this would be the only way she could do her part in paying forward their kindness.

"I'm sorry, please bear with me." Shawn now had a letter from Trisha that he had to read. It was addressed to them all, except Mitch, but Shawn wanted him to hear this.

To the only family who has ever made me feel wanted and loved.

Dear Peter and Sharon,

    I want you to know that I have always felt that you were my parents, and in my make-believe world that I had lived for so long, your kindness and love saw me through. I want to thank you for loving me and for all you gave me, especially your unconditional love. I will always be grateful.
    You would be the only grandparents I would wish for to be in my daughter's life. I know that she will learn the true meaning of love from the pair of you as I had.
    I know that if you are reading this, it will not be an easy time for any of you, and that I am sorry for. You know I loved you with all my heart, and thank you for being there for me, and now for my daughter.

Love,
Trisha

Dear Jessy,

    It breaks my heart to know that you are now being read my letter. The one thing I'm not sorry for is having the one person in my life who taught me what sisters were really all about. I could not have asked for a better sister, blood or not. Jessy, I know the pain you must be feeling right now. Please know I'm okay and I will be waiting anxiously to see you again.

I have always looked up to you. When I told you about being pregnant, you told me to hold on to my pride and to be proud of who I was. Having a baby was a blessing sent to us by God and that you would always be there for my baby and me. So it is with great regret yet with all the love I have in my heart that I ask this of you.

Please, please, Jessy, take my baby and raise her with all the same values and love that your parents raised you and me. Shawn and I have discussed this to great lengths, and we had both agreed that if I were ever to die while our baby was young, we would both want you to take her and raise her as your own. She will need a loving woman in her life. I had no one else to ask other than your mom, but they have raised their daughter and I didn't think it would be fair to ask them to take my daughter this late in their lives. But I would know that Crystal would be loved by the woman who is caring for her, and she would have loving grandparents.

Please, Jessy, I don't want her ending up in the hands of my parents or social services.

Shawn is tied up at work too much to try and care for our daughter.

The only thing I will ask of you is to please allow Shawn to see her whenever he can and to share her life with you.

Shawn will not stand in the way of Crystal's care although you have to know he loves his daughter sincerely. I know this is tearing him apart and his

ROAD SIDE CROSSES

heart is also breaking at this time. I only wish I could ease all your pain.

Please do this for me so I may rest in peace knowing my daughter has the best of care from her aunt, Jessy, as well as her father and her grandparents, Peter and Sharon.

I thank you from the bottom of my heart, and I hope that God will guide you in the decisions you have to make. Please know that I will love you and watch over you always.

Love, your little sister and best friend,
Trisha

With the will and letter read, they took turns blowing their noses and wiping away the tears. Shawn sat with his head hung and shoulders slouched like a man with an extra heavy load upon them.

Sharon was wrapped in Peter's arms, sobbing into his chest.

Mitch had Jessy wrapped in his arms, listening to her sob. This played hell on him. There was so much pain in this room. It wouldn't matter where you moved; it had a hold of you.

Shawn got up and went over to Trisha. He picked up her lifeless hand and kissed it as he said, "Okay, sweetheart. I have done what you asked me to. Now it is out of my hands. We will wait together."

The doctor had come in as Shawn had requested, and he had shown them Trisha's will. Once the doctor was satisfied that Shawn was the one to execute her will, he got the ball rolling for the organ harvest. Whenever they used those two words together, Shawn wanted to throw up. But it was her last request, and no matter how he felt, he would see it through.

Jessy went over to Shawn and sat down beside him. She reached for his hand, and he had a look of indifference on his face, almost a frown.

"Shawn, as much as I love Crystal and Trisha, I don't see how I would be any better for her than what you have to offer her. I have a full-time job, and I would have to use day care. I really don't know much about being a mother. Besides, you are her father. Would it not be better if you were in her life all the time or as much as possible?"

"My job keeps me away so much she would hardly see me. Besides, she needs a woman in her life. What do I know about girl things?"

"Do you not have anyone there that could help you?"

"Jessy, I would have to have her in day care, being raised by a stranger in a strange place. It would not be a family setting or a home setting. I don't want that for my little girl. Trisha did not want that. What else am I to do?" He ran his fingers through his hair as he sat with his head in his hands. Then he said, "Would you take a couple of days and think about it, please? I will pay you whatever you need to take care of my little girl."

At that moment, Jessy's heart went out to him. "Okay, let me think about it. This was so unexpected. It's a little overwhelming, losing Trisha and now this. I do need time to think."

Shawn nodded then said, "They will be shutting the machine off late tomorrow. There are sick people waiting for organs, and I don't want to see Trisha lying like this any longer. Crystal will be discharged then."

"I understand." Jessy looked at Sharon, and Sharon was standing as stiff as a stone. Going over to her, Jessy asked, "Mom, are you all right?"

With a tear in her eye about to fall, Sharon reached out and put her hand on Jessy's arm as she said, "Jessy."

"I know, Mom." Jessy walked away. She had to clear her mind. She had to think.

"Oh, God, what am I to do?" She found herself in Crystal's room. Crystal was sleeping, and as she stood there admiring that precious little girl, it was as if a weight had just been lifted off her shoulders. She looked around with the feeling there was someone else in the room with her. Then she heard, *"Please do this for me, for Crystal."*

"What?" Jessy turned completely around, but there was no one there. She could have sworn that was Trisha talking to her. Putting her hands on to the side of the crib, it was like a wave of emotions hit her. This little girl needed her as her mother had needed Sharon. Could she make it work? Jessy knew her parents would give her all the help they could. But would that be enough. Could she give Crystal everything love had to offer?

At that moment, she felt a hand come down on her shoulder. She reached up and put her hand on top. She knew it was Mitch without looking.

"Oh, Mitch, I don't know what to do. This little girl needs me, but I don't know anything about being a mother, a parent. How do I raise a baby alone?"

"Jessy you don't have to."

Looking at Mitch with a frown, she said, "What do you mean?"

"Your parents will gladly help you, and if you were to become my wife, I then could help you. Not that I wouldn't anyway, but just think, she would have both of us all the time. Then you could put your work off until she was in school, the way Emily did." He had just taken her breath away and didn't even realize it.

"Did you just ask me to marry you?"

"Yes, I did, and it's something I have wanted to ask you for a very long time. You know how they say you wait for the right moment? Well, I believe this is the right moment. Jessy, I have loved you from Day 1. I knew that you loved your work and never wanted to mix work with a relationship, so I stayed a friend, but a friend that loves you sincerely. I also think that it's time for us to become one and take this little girl and make a family with her. Jessy, she needs us. Shawn needs us to do this." Then he stopped and looked at her. He thought he knew her, but just maybe he had misread her, so he thought he had better ask.

"Jessy, you do have feelings for me, don't you?"

A little shocked by this whole turn of events had her feeling a little off-kilter.

"Jess."

As she brought herself back into focus, a smile spread across her face, and it lit up as she folded herself into Mitch's arms. "Of course I have feelings for you, Mitch, but marriage?"

"I'm sorry, Jess. I don't want to just shack up. I think that your parents would be totally disgusted with me as a man if I didn't show their daughter enough respect to marry her."

Jessy looked up at Mitch, and he saw the sparkle in her eyes. At that moment, he knew what Peter was talking about.

"Oh, Mitch, I have loved you forever. Yes, I would love to be your wife."

Kissing to seal their agreement, Mitch then said, "Let's go tell the others and see if we can make something good come out of all this tragedy."

Although it broke the hearts around her as Trisha's life had ended, they could only pray that the choices they made were the right ones. As one life ends, tomorrow, many got a new beginning.

CPSIA information can be obtained at www.ICGtesting.com
Printed in the USA
LVOW100524080513

332721LV00003B/14/P

9 781479 791873